A Peek Inside

In that moment, he couldn't remember his manners. He hadn't the patience to woo her gently.

He kissed her.

Hard. Quick. Desperate to convince his soul the woman he loved yet lived.

She must've been in shock. She stood, stiff in his arms while he kissed her like a brute.

A second passed and his conscience nearly convinced him he'd gone about this all wrong.

But then, all of a sudden, she kissed him back. Her arm looped around his neck as she pulled his head down and leveraged herself up higher to meet him. He nearly laughed aloud as she used his boots for a step-stool.

His heart sang with arresting joy and he lost himself in the eagerness of her kiss.

"Lizzy—"

Her kiss claimed his mouth again, in two short bursts. "I'm mad at you."

originally published within
a collection of five novellas titled

Gunsmoke & Gingham
exclusively for kindle

on February 14, 2017

by agreement with the cooperative authors:
Kirsten Osbourne
Peggy L. Henderson
Amelia C. Adams
Margery Scott

Praise For

THE
GUNSMITH'S
Bride

"This is a nice, clean set of western historical romance novellas (GUNSMOKE & GINGHAM). My favorite was The Gunsmith's Bride by Kristin Holt. The scenario of how Morgan and Elizabeth meet was quite interesting."

~ Susa, Amazon Reviewer, 5 stars

"This was a great story. I loved that I hated Lizzy's mom at first. Morgan was the perfect hero. I was surprised by what happened between Morgan's dad and Lizzy's mom. The shooting and ensuing problems were done just right."

~ Phyllis H, Amazon Reviewer, 5 stars

"I purchased this for Kristin Holt's story, "The Gunsmith's Bride." I loved it!"
  ~ Sara, Goodreads Reviewer, 3 Goodreads Stars

"Nice clean stories. I enjoyed this collection [GUNSMOKE & GINGHAM]. They were fun, wholesome and something I would recommend to anyone, even my mother! thanks for the lovely reading!"
  ~ Angela, Goodreads Reviewer, 4 Goodreads Stars

"The Gunsmith's Bride by Kristin Holt. Kristin writes the sweetest romances. Loveable, sensitive heroes and sweet but not weak heroines. This one has two romances, one heroine I wasn't sure about, but ended up loving at the end. Two heroes, two heroines, a very enjoyable read."
  ~ Arlene J.E., Amazon Reviewer, 5 stars

"The Gunsmith's Bride by Kristin Holt. I'm always impressed with how well-written Kristin Holt's stories are! This is really a story of first impressions, too. I did not like Zylphia, Morgan's dad's mail-order bride at the start at all! There are also little bits of humor in this story, like Hannah [Elizabeth] was "26 years of age & firmly on the shelf..." I really enjoyed this story!"
  ~ Kindle Customer, Amazon Reviewer, 5 stars

THE
GUNSMITH'S
Bride

Copy Edit by RVP The Man Editing:
https://RVPTheManEditing.weebly.com/

Cover art copyright © 2018 by Kelli Ann at Inspire Creative Services: www.InspireCreativeServices.com/

THE GUNSMITH'S *Bride*

Morgan Hudson can't begrudge his widowed father a second chance at happiness. So when Dad's mail-order bride arrives in Mountain Home with a beautiful daughter, Morgan's life flips upside down. The lovesick fifty-year-olds need a chaperone, and Morgan can't remember to treat Lizzy like a sister. Will their emergent love survive their parents' romance, threats from the past, and a law forbidding kissing on the streets of Mountain Home?

Can Morgan welcome the same difficult woman as stepmother and mother-in-law?

Dedication

For the real Elizabeth Louise, "Favorite Cousin
Lizzy". Thank you for loaning me your name.
Wishing you the beauty of your own happily ever
after with a hero even better than Morgan Hudson.

THE GUNSMITH'S Bride

A Sweet Western Historical Mail-Order Bride
Romance Novella
(Rated PG)
Holidays in Mountain Home, Book 6

by

USA TODAY Bestselling Author

KRISTIN HOLT

The books in this series are loosely connected and may be read in any order.

To hear about New Releases, Special Sales,
and *receive a FREE novella*,
Sign up for Kristin Holt's Newsletter.

www.KristinHolt.com/newsletter

Note: Kristin is <u>e-free</u>

One

Mountain Home, Colorado
June 1885

"Son, I've decided to marry the woman I've been writing."

Morgan Hudson paused in the smooth, rhythmic motions of sweeping the workshop floor. He'd known this decision would be coming. He'd seen Dad's smile when pale blue, floral-scented stationery arrived in the mail. The old man deserved happiness wherever he found it.

Morgan shook himself and resumed sweeping. Dad wouldn't look Morgan in the eye while admitting another woman would take Mama's place, so no sense looking up from the chore. He pushed the business-end of the broom beneath the workbench and caught curls of English walnut and chips of maple.

He drew deeply, inhaling scents of gun oil, seasoned wood, and freshly cut grass. The windows stood open to allow the evening breeze through the shop. Familiar scents. Comforting. Perfect, just as it was.

His days working in comfortable silence side by side with his father were numbered.

A woman had come between them, just like he'd known she would. At least that woman wasn't Arrah Cresswell. Thank God for that small favor.

"Congratulations." Morgan squatted and swept the leavings into the dustpan. "I'm glad it worked out."

Dad continued reassembling the Colt .45, his hands moving with surety and confidence bred into him. He'd learned the trade from Grandpa before him, who'd learned from his father. Four generations of Hudsons smithed the finest guns— and repaired every make.

Not for the first time, he was grateful Dad had taught him everything there was to know. He'd rather be a gunsmith than a farmer any day of the week.

Long streams of sunlight poured through west-facing windows. This time of night, mothers called their little ones in for supper. Fathers made their way home from the fields or the shops. Families gathered for a meal around the table.

For three years, it'd been just Dad and Morgan. For a while, he'd believed Arrah would join them, that he'd be the one to take a wife. But now the bride would be Mrs.—

Star? Spar? *Speare.* That was it. Speare. With an 'e'.

"When will Mrs. Speare arrive?" He set the broom and dustpan in their place.

"Next Wednesday." Dad finished the reassembly, tested the movement, and wiped excess oil from his hands with a cloth.

Five days. Dad had known for at least a week. Why hadn't he said anything?

Dad looked up, sunlight glinting off his eyeglasses. "It's time you marry."

"No, thanks." The thought of marriage gave him a gut ache. *Any* reminder of Arrah gave him a gut ache.

"You're twenty-eight."

"Only twenty-seven." Dad had turned fifty in March. Simple arithmetic.

"Your birthday's around the corner. You're losing daylight."

"Tried that route, remember? Didn't work out so well."

"Marriage worked out mighty fine for your mother and me. You just need to find the right woman. Get back on the horse, so to speak."

"Maybe I'll find her. Someday." A load of hogwash and they both knew it, but no sense arguing over something that wouldn't change. "If she's in Mountain Home, I haven't noticed her."

"You ought to take up a correspondence courtship."

Just because Dad had found his bride-to-be that way didn't mean Morgan could. "No, thanks."

"I thought we'd move into the first house, give her and her children privacy in the new house."

Just like Dad to change the subject when Morgan dug in and held his ground. As an only child, and his father's apprentice, he'd spent more time alone with his Dad by age twelve than most boys did through their entire lives.

"Figured so." The new conversation path suited him fine.

The first house—the one-room cabin Dad had built upon arriving in Mountain Home had kept their family snug from winter's storms and comfortably cool in summer's heat. They'd moved into the big house less than two years before Mama took sick with the cancer that slowly drained her of life. She'd lived in that two story, wood frame, upright and wing construction for only four years.

She'd been so proud of the proper house, but refused to allow Dad and Morgan to turn the first house into a shed. *Consider the memories inside these four walls.*

Three years gone, and he could still hear his mother's voice in his memory. Fading, sure, but still there. He liked the idea of living in the old place, nearer to her. It'd be like coming home. No hardship at all.

Morgan shut the two windows, latching each with care. "Children, huh?"

Dad nodded.

"How many?"

"Two. Boy and girl."

Morgan couldn't picture children in the house, the clatter of button-up shoes on the stairs and the ring of little voices. Just 'cause he'd never had children around didn't mean he wouldn't get used to it.

Or maybe he'd remain in the first house and give the new family privacy well after the wedding. Living with Dad and his new wife, along with her children—and more babies?—no, thank you.

The last of the tools put away, the workshop put to rights, Dad opened the back door on soundless hinges and removed the key ring from his pocket. He locked up tight.

They walked side by side along the path through the lot, past the shed, a carriage house and barn, alongside laundry drying in the breeze, past the kitchen garden Ina kept tidied of weeds and producing until the hard frost.

Nothing more to say, but they didn't need to.

Dad had been gloriously happy, married to Mama, and he intended to be happily married once more. The plans were set in motion. In his twenty-eighth year, he knew loneliness and just might consider his father's suggestion...if Arrah hadn't left such a bad taste in his mouth.

Five more days. Given the weekend, and the train arriving at four on Wednesday afternoon like clockwork, that meant three more days alone with Dad in the shop.

Three days until his relationship with Dad changed forever.

Elizabeth Speare longed for the final leg of the journey to end.

Less than two hours, and they'd arrive, finally, in Mountain Home. She could stand *anything* for two hours, couldn't she?

The train car rocked in time to the incessant clatter of wheels. Summertime heat made the shut-in space miserable, and amplified gnawing hunger pangs. Everyone aboard was uncomfortable—but only Mother complained. Well, her mother and a pair of exhausted children across the aisle. The little ones tussled, chattered, cried, and fought over toys. They'd grown more and more irritable since Denver.

"Those *dreadful* children." Mother complained every few minutes, rehashing the same ten irritants, ensuring the misery of everyone else. One by one, the other passengers had tiptoed to vacant seats farther away. Mother hadn't noticed.

Two hours. Only two more hours. "Mother, I'll go to the dining car and buy us something cool to eat. Maybe they have ice for your beverage. You'd like that."

"Stay, Elizabeth Louise." She rearranged the damp handkerchief on her forehead. "Don't leave me. I can't bear to be alone."

She shut her eyes against the urge to scream. *Why* had she agreed to accompany Mother west?

"Why is it unbearably hot in this car?" Mother shifted, as if trying to find a more comfortable position.

The little boys tangled into a knot, the eldest punching the little brother—a toddler of no more than two. Their mother, an olive-toned, brunette beauty remained pleasant, despite her children's distress at being cooped up in a hot train. She displayed unfailing patience with her little ones. And a cranky old woman.

In contrast, Zylphia Speare was short tempered and impossible to please—especially when stressed.

The closer they drew to Mountain Home and Mother's husband-to-be, the more insufferable she became. If Elizabeth were the bride, she imagined she'd be nervous. At twenty-six years of age and firmly on the shelf, what did she know of bridal jitters?

"My head," Mother simpered. "The dreadful pounding won't leave me in peace."

The young mother leaned forward, bright blue feathers on her stylish hat waving with the sway of the train. "I'm sorry to trouble you," she whispered, "but I need assistance."

Elizabeth owed the woman a peace offering. She glanced at the children just as the bigger one bellowed—the baby had knotted a fist in his brother's hair and pulled. "Help?"

"My name is Mrs. Felicity Gideon."

"Miss Elizabeth Speare."

"Would you be so kind to tend my sons, please, while I hurry to the dining car? They wouldn't eat when we stopped in Denver. If I feed them, they'll settle down. Maybe sleep."

"They're so *noisy*." Mother shifted her handkerchief upon her brow. "*My* children were angels. Never made such a deplorable racket."

Mrs. Gideon winked at Elizabeth in good humor. Near Elizabeth's age, she traveled without husband or nanny. Her children were handfuls—expensively dressed handfuls. Wrestling them all the way to the dining car and back wouldn't be easy. "Of course, yes, Mrs. Gideon. I'll help."

Mother whipped the sodden hankie off her brow. "If you're tending those terrors, Elizabeth Louise, you cannot tend to me."

Elizabeth counted to five, then to ten, urging her temper to cool. "Mother, I've done everything either of us can think of. If I sit with the boys and tell them a story, you'll have more space."

"Do make the wretches stop their infernal

fussing." Mother covered her eyes with the lace-trimmed linen.

Elizabeth stood just as the other woman rose. "You'll hurry back?"

"Immediately." She smoothed her fashionable skirts, blue silk embroidery on cream cotton. "In payment, I'll bring you and your mother a bite to eat."

Food! Gratitude swelled. She quickly removed a half-dollar from her reticule.

"I couldn't eat a morsel!" Mother pressed a hand to her slender midsection. "The ceaseless rocking of this coach has upset my delicate digestion."

Elizabeth's hunger was the only misery she could do anything about. "Thank you." She tried to press the coin into the other woman's hand.

"No, no. My treat. As thanks for giving me two minutes to myself."

She indicated her sons with a tip of her chin, but they both knew she included Zylphia Speare. With a quick smile, she hurried up the aisle.

Elizabeth sat. The boys quieted long enough to take her in with big brown eyes. Their dark hair stood on end, as Mrs. Gideon had never combed it. Perspiration dampened their hairline and reddened their cherub cheeks.

The little one tucked a thumb into his mouth.

"Who are you?" the bigger one asked.

"I'm Elizabeth."

"*Do* stop prattling on." Mother again. And her blasted sick headache. And her nerves. And the heat.

Elizabeth glanced up the aisle at Mrs. Felicity Gideon's retreating back and prayed she returned.

Two

Against his better judgment, Morgan joined his father at the train station to collect Mrs. Speare and her children.

Dad had closed the gunsmith shop early and asked Morgan to come along to help lift the trunks into the wagon, but Morgan saw through all that.

If all Dad needed was Morgan at his side, in order to greet his bride with confidence, that he could do. And pretend to be happy.

Dad clutched the cabinet card of his bride, studied the image, then the disembarking passengers. "That's her. There. In gray."

Willow slim, in a simple, dove-gray dress and standing on the platform. Dad's bride clutched the hands of two small children. Naughty children, who fought with all their might to free themselves of her grip.

Morgan wasn't so sure, not without a clear look at her face. She bent to say something to the older of the two, then straightened, and he caught a glimpse of light brown hair tucked beneath her far from fashionable hat. One of those styles worn by old, penny-pinching ladies.

Dad's bride might dress like an old woman, but she wasn't old.

She lifted her chin, scanned the crowd, and yes, he was right. Youthful, fresh of face and figure. Not what a man wanted to see—his dad's bride, not a day older than himself. Probably younger.

And *lovely*.

Immediate attraction warred with wariness. Same build as Arrah, same feminine grace.

"Her?" Morgan pointed, disliking her already. "How old is Mrs. Speare?"

Dad shrugged and tapped a finger on the face of the cabinet card. "That's her, all right."

Morgan clamped his jaw. Why hadn't Dad asked *important* questions—*like her age*—before proposing marriage and bringing her to Colorado?

One of the miscreants hanging from Mrs. Speare's hand broke free and ran. Before he'd made it two steps, she caught him around the middle and sat herself squarely on the platform, both children locked in the circle of her arms, upon her lap.

Not Arrah-like at all.

First, Arrah never would've tended her own children. Second, Arrah never, *never* would have *sat* upon the platform.

Morgan nudged through the crowd, Dad close behind. No matter what the woman was or wasn't, she needed assistance.

Two men blocked Morgan's view, one of them settling a bowler upon his pate. Conversations swelled all around them. The train whistled a shrill blast.

The crowd thinned, and they finally reached her side. Morgan instantly dropped to his haunches and, thinking only of helping, moved to take one of the children. He pulled up short. No mother would hand off her child to a stranger.

Mrs. Speare looked up and smiled. Warm and genuine, an open smile that punched him hard in his gut.

Stepmother-to-be. He clamped his jaw and fought to break eye contact.

Thankfully, her gaze quickly darted to Dad. "Hello, Mr. Hudson. I recognize you from the photograph you sent." She smiled at him, every bit as warmly and genuinely as she had smiled at Morgan.

He hated himself for feeling jealousy for Dad's good fortune.

This whole thing—Mrs. Speare, in the house, in his father's life—would not be easy.

One of the children wrested free from his mother's hold. Morgan caught him easily and swung him onto his shoulders and caught his bowler as it tumbled. "Hold on, little man. You're not going anywhere."

The child held on tight—nearly pulling Morgan's hair out by the roots.

And Mrs. Speare looked from the child on his shoulders to Morgan, smiling like an angel.

Perfect teeth. White. He adjusted his initial assessment. This woman *couldn't* be mid-twenties. Barely twenty. Plenty of childbearing years before her. He'd known Mama and Dad had wanted more children—was that why Dad had intentionally chosen a much younger bride?

Morgan would move out.

In with the child-bride and out with the twenty-seven-year-old son. He didn't know where he'd go, not yet, but he'd go. Quickly. The first house wasn't far enough. He'd find a room in town. And stay away. Far away, from his much too-lovely stepmother.

"Thank you, sir." Her smile widened, deepened, and caught him with another quick jab to the gut. "You must be Morgan." She turned back to Dad with ease. "Mr. Hudson, my mother will join us shortly. She needed a moment to compose herself."

Her *mother*?

Dad had been willing to take on a bride with two children, but *three* generations moving in? All at the same time? A *mother-in-law*? Morgan expected distress on Dad's face, but he merely reached for the smaller child, nestled the monster on his arm and offered Mrs. Speare a hand up from the platform floor.

"Oh, thank you." She stood easily, in a whoosh of gray skirts...and barely reached Morgan's shoulder—uh, *Dad's* shoulder.

One look at Dad and his bride, side by side, and he knew—with unshakable confidence—the two were horribly mismatched. What man, fifty years of age married a twenty-year-old? Yes, discordant marriages happened all the time. Young women wanted men who were settled, had made their way in life, could offer a comfortable living.

The naughty boy on his shoulders fought for

freedom. "Mama!" He nearly dove off Morgan's shoulders, reaching hard, but not toward Mrs. Speare.

The little fellow reached for Rocky Gideon's wife, Felicity.

He should have recognized those little rascals, spitting images of their father. Rocky had brought them into the shop last week.

Felicity, dressed in blue and cream and the high fashions Morgan had learned to recognize because of Arrah, reached for the boy. "There you are. Were you good for Miss Speare?"

Miss Speare?

Relief—no, *not* relief!—recoiled like an old .50 Hawken. He did *not* want to hope this young woman wasn't committed to marry Dad.

"He wasn't any trouble at all." *Miss* Speare greeted Felicity as if they were friends—had they met on the train?

"Hello, Mr. Hudson, Morgan." Felicity set her son on his feet and reached for the little guy Dad held. "Give Mama a kiss."

The boy plastered a wet kiss to Felicity's cheek.

Miss Speare asked, "You caught the baggage handler in time?"

"I did. Thank you for watching them. Gentlemen, thank you for helping. Say good-bye, children. We'll call on you soon, Elizabeth. Good-bye Mr. Hudson, Morgan." Felicity turned toward the street, "Oh, there's your mother now."

Felicity called to her husband and hurried to meet him. Morgan would've said hello to his friend and customer, but the woman disembarking in a flash of immense purple in the sunlight, snared him and wouldn't let go.

Purple hat. Purple silk dress.

And not in an appealing way.

For *Pete's sake*.

Morgan cleared his throat and clapped Dad on the back. "*That* is Mrs. Speare."

Disoriented, Dad consulted the picture. Compared the woman destroying the color purple for everyone else, to the girl in gray who closely resembled her, to the portrait and back again.

Mother and daughter. Had to be.

"Oh, good," Dad murmured. "Very good."

"There she is, now." The young, flaxen haired woman nodded at the woman dressed from head to toe in garish purple. The hue might be acceptable for a widow's late mourning, but complimentary to her pale skin and hair the same color as her daughter's? No.

Arrah had taught him many things, the least of which was a thing or two about fashion and a woman's duty to dress to best set off her features. Arrah's white-blonde beauty had been showcased in palest of greens, blues, and pinks. Never had she worn anything so tasteless.

Mrs. Speare and purple got along as well as Morgan and Arrah—which meant not at all. The jet black of full mourning would have done her no favors.

Dad didn't seem to notice. He doffed his hat, held it over his heart, and took in Mrs. Speare. "Zylphia?"

"George?"

Dad nodded and offered his hand.

The woman, Zylphia Speare, gushed. Simpered. Smiled—but not as lovely as her daughter's.

For Pete's sake—making a grown man watch his father's courtship was wrong on so many levels.

The introductions went all around. "Mr. Hudson and Mr. Hudson, may I present my daughter, Miss Elizabeth Louise Speare."

Ah, so the young one was a *Miss* Speare. Rocky's wife hadn't been mistaken.

"Your letter said you'd bring two children?" Morgan couldn't help but ask. He'd expected two children—and that had led to an unnecessary and uncomfortable span. He needed justification.

Elizabeth held his gaze, and slipped her arm through her mother's...for support? "My brother decided to remain behind in St. Louis."

"I see." But he didn't.

Children? Who called a woman in her twenties a child? Just how old was this brother?

Befuddlement must've shown because Elizabeth filled in the blanks. "My brother is a carpenter, a journeyman with a successful furniture-building company. He thought it best to remain in the city."

"Welcome to Mountain Home." Dad took Elizabeth's hand. "It's a pleasure to have you join us. This is my son, Morgan."

The girl smiled. *Again.*

Mrs. Speare leapt into the conversation's lull. "We'll be the happiest of families." She opened her arms—silently demanding a hug. From *him*.

Morgan backed up a step, the thought of embracing Dad's bride a horror he'd failed to anticipate.

"Oh, stop," she chided. "Don't be shy, young man." She looped her arms about his neck and pulled his spine into a bow. She enveloped him in a cloud of floral perfume.

He nearly choked. He didn't like *anyone* too close, and didn't enjoy the casual touch of friends. This woman, a complete stranger, ran amok over every boundary, everything comfortable. She'd offended, in too many ways to count. If not for Dad, he'd break her hold and put distance between them.

"You and I," she said, her face far too close to his, "will be the *best* of friends, you and I. Mother and son. You *must* call me Mother."

Three

Back at the house, Morgan helped Dad unload the wagon. He carried trunks and valises upstairs, and crates into the kitchen.

The faster Morgan unloaded the ladies' belongings, the faster he could escape. Dad no doubt wanted to make his new family's acquaintance. And Morgan wanted air. And peace.

The mere fact that Dad's bride *ordered* him to address her as Mother meant he couldn't. *Wouldn't.* Not e*ver.*

He would decide how he'd address the woman, if at all.

He'd just cleared the kitchen door to fetch the last trunk when Ray strode through the back lot, by way of the shop.

Ray Cresswell—more friend than cousin—waved. "Why is the shop closed at half-past four?"

His dark hair shone with a flash of red in summer sunlight.

"Company arrived on the train."

Ray hefted the other end of the particularly large, heavy trunk. Between the two of them, they wrestled it up the stairs and into the bedroom Dad had shared with Mama.

Ray swept off his hat, mopped his forearm over his brow, took in the myriad trunks, and glared at Morgan. "What company stays in the master bedroom?"

Not a discussion to have in the house. Not now. "Come on."

Morgan thumped down the stairs, glad to see the women and Dad were in the parlor so he wouldn't have to stop to introduce Ray. His cousin had a way of speaking his mind, and until he understood the situation, no one wanted to know what Ray thought.

Morgan opened the back door before he realized Ray hadn't followed.

His cousin had halted at the base of the stairs, staring into the parlor. Captivated by the hideous purple get-up or the lovely vision in gray.

Morgan figured he knew which had snared Ray's attention.

"Come on." Morgan repeated, grabbed Ray by the arm, and shooed him outside. He headed for the wagon and waiting team.

Ray whistled through his teeth, Ray's patented expression of appreciation every time he admired a beautiful woman. If Morgan had heard it once, he'd heard it a thousand times.

"Who is she?" Morgan vaulted into the wagon.

Morgan untied the reins from the brake handle, clicked his tongue, flicked the reins. "Dad's company."

Ray's infatuation soured to distrust. "Why is a pretty filly like that visiting your pa?"

How to answer that? By the time they'd pulled up to the carriage house, Morgan had opted for direct and blunt. "Her mother's engaged to be married. To Dad."

Ray whirled. "Since when?"

"Don't know. A few months. They've been writing."

"You know what this'll do to my mother?"

He could imagine. "Dad's a grown man. He makes his own decisions."

"Am I supposed to be happy my uncle, my *widower uncle*—up and forgets Aunt Tillie to marry somebody else?"

"Mama's gone. Nothing can change that."

"It's too soon." Ray shoved off the seat, bouncing the rig in his anger.

The conversation seemed over, until Morgan had the second horse unhitched, the wagon stowed, and had taken a curry comb to the team.

"You know what?" Ray demanded, "Mama still cries at night for her sister. It ain't right of Uncle George to forget the bride of his youth."

"I know." He doubted Dad had forgotten. But a new wife would change things.

"How long have you known 'bout this?"

Two more long strokes of the comb. "A few days."

"Why didn't you tell me?"

"Couldn't think about it, much less speak of it." He stilled, finding comfort in the steady horse beneath his hands. "Now we both know. Dad's ready to marry again. He's chosen Mrs. Speare."

Minutes passed. He took up his comb again, stroking in soothing arcs.

"Mrs. Speare? The young one or the old hag in purple?" Shades of the carefree Ray showed through.

"The elder. In purple." He coughed to hide a grin. "The younger one is Miss Elizabeth Speare."

"Available, is she?"

Morgan shrugged, not liking his cousin's interest. Not at all.

"Wait—unless you've already claimed her."

"What? No. *No.*" The idea thrilled *and* chilled. "The girl's my stepsister. Or will be." He'd have to be insane to want Mrs. Speare as stepmother *and* mother-in-law.

Ray nodded toward the house. "I might have to pay the pretty lady a visit."

On their first evening in the Hudson home, Elizabeth kept her smile tacked in place as long as she could manage. She wanted nothing more than to claim exhaustion, retire from this "First Family Supper", as Mother had deemed it, and retire.

The dining room was nicely appointed, the chairs comfortable. Mother was in one of her better moods, enjoying Mr. Hudson's full attention. Mother had seated herself at Mr. Hudson's left, leaving Elizabeth and Morgan to fend for themselves.

"Do tell me more," Mother urged Mr. Hudson. "I'm enraptured with everything about you."

The conversation had dragged on like this for a half hour. Mr. Hudson happily answering every question, and Mother's conversation skills making a fine showing—if ignoring her daughter and soon-to-be stepson didn't count.

Elizabeth sipped cold well water, far too aware of Morgan Hudson on her right. He sat at the foot of the table, his presence immense. And tension-filled. He didn't like her, or Mother, and utterly distrusted them both. That was evident in each glance and in every vigorous stroke of knife through beefsteak.

What a disaster. Why must *he* be the first man to turn her head?

Of course, she'd noticed men before Morgan Hudson. But he'd been the first to truly captivate her.

If she'd arrived without her mother, she might've had the *slightest* of chances with Morgan. But not now.

He, naturally, would never be remotely interested in her, if only because of their parents.

Parents who got along swimmingly and seemed to adore one another. Their correspondence had been going on for months, introducing them thoroughly, but the magnitude of the lovers' affection had accelerated much faster than Elizabeth could have supposed.

Behind the swinging door into the kitchen, a crash of shattering dishes erupted.

"Heaven's Angels!" Mother jumped, her hand at her throat. "What on earth?"

Both Hudson men eyed the door into the kitchen. Morgan's brows drew together. He chewed, dropped his napkin beside his plate, and had just pushed back his chair as if to check on the housekeeper when the woman erupted through the swinging door separating kitchen and dining room. The door banged against the wall. Her chest heaved with labored breaths.

Elizabeth stilled.

The woman had been cold and unpleasant from the moment Mr. Hudson had made introductions. Unhappy to hear "we're having company for dinner, five in all" meant two ladies were joining them.

Well, if not from announcement of guests for supper, then from the moment she learned the guests would be staying indefinitely.

What was the woman's name? Oh, yes. Ina... Her surname started with a D, but Elizabeth couldn't recall. She knew Mother's moods intimately, knew precisely what to do to ease the tensions, but this—*this* was a whole new ball of wax.

Mother set her fork down with precision and straightened her spine further. "Do we have a problem, Miss Dimond?"

Elizabeth had seen Mother's Imperial Empress routine a time or three. Ina didn't deserve it.

"Yes, *we* have a problem!"

"I will deduct the cost of the dishes from your pay."

Ina's cheeks, red with anger, mottled. "You haven't authority—"

"You are fired." Mother's tone remained even and moderate. "You will leave my home within sixty seconds."

The housekeeper—the *former* housekeeper— gasped, shrieked with outrage, and pushed back through the still-swinging door.

The wall clock ticked louder than ever.

Embarrassed, Elizabeth couldn't look at either Hudson, as both men remained frozen, as if stunned by Mother's incredible overreach. *Her* home? No wedding had occurred. Mr. Hudson could easily decide Mother wasn't the right match, might dismiss *them*—

Mother set her hand upon Mr. Hudson's fist on the tabletop. "A woman must control the domestics in her home. I *will* have respect from the help."

Miss Dimond returned through the door, sending it crashing once more. Her reticule swung from one wrist and a serviceable parasol clutched like a bludgeon. "I've kept house for the Hudsons for years!" She pointed her parasol at Morgan, jabbed as if to wound. "Since your mama took sick. Two long years I nursed her, while cancer grew in her belly. I loved your mother. I treated *you* like my own. And *you*, George, I treated you like family."

The poor woman was bushwhacked by sudden introduction of a bride from St. Louis.

That explained much.

Familiar, painful empathy flooded Elizabeth. Ina had filled her labor for the Hudsons with love, lived like his wife...but not.

Morgan threw his napkin onto his plate, and shoved back his chair, and rose to his considerable height.

Ina stopped him with both hands raised. "What do I get for my trouble? Nothing. Only news of five, maybe six for supper. Do I see five or six? No, I see four."

This wasn't about food prepared. This was about the guest list. And Mother's chair slid indecently close to George Hudson at the head of the table.

"You owe me two months' salary, *George*." Ina vibrated with anger. "Full wages. This...*this woman* brought plenty in those crates. Ordered me to wash them, and dry them, without a single water spot."

Elizabeth saw straight through the woman's fury to the pain beneath. She'd called him by his first name, leaning heavily on the familiarity. The woman who'd kept house for George Hudson all these years was *in love* with him. Probably had been since she'd come to work for him. All while nursing his dying wife, scrubbing his floors, cooking his meals, washing his clothes.

With dignity in every step, Ina Dimond exited, but not through the kitchen door as she probably did every evening on her way home. She marched through the reception hall, and out the front door, leaving it open wide.

Morgan remained standing, barely containing his anger.

Mother cleared her throat delicately and folded her hands in her lap. "That was most unpleasant, but necessary. I assure you it was necessary."

But George Hudson, man of the house, surprised her. "Yes. I apologize, Mrs. Speare. That was—"

"No need to apologize." Mother smiled brightly, as if she hadn't a kitchen to put to rights, as if the front door weren't hanging open for all the neighborhood to see.

"Excuse me." Morgan tucked his chair beneath the table with complete control. Even his voice sounded calm and steady. "I've lost my appetite." He exited, following Miss Dimond as if nothing untoward had happened. As if she'd simply said goodnight and gone on her way, and he realized she'd left her shawl behind.

Nothing wrong with us.

No, not here. Everything is fine. Perfectly normal.

Elizabeth wanted to silently disappear.

Any minute, Mr. Hudson would chastise Mother, put her in her place, stand and rail at her impudence.

But he didn't. He held Mother's hand, soothed her. "Hire another housekeeper of your own choosing."

"Geo, I'd rather cook for you, myself."

Geo. The personal nickname grated, chafed. Father had been in the ground *six months*. Mother wasn't out of mourning. Crepe would have still draped the house, covered every window, had they not sold it in preparation for moving to Mountain Home.

Too soon.

As if Elizabeth didn't exist, Mr. Hudson searched Mother's eyes. "Miss Dimond kept the houses clean. Cooked three meals a day. Did the laundry. That's all far too much for you."

"I'm accustomed to all of that and more." Mother patted Mr. Hudson's hands, clasped together about hers. "Houses?"

"The first house, out back. Morgan and I

moved back in yesterday. Propriety, until the wedding."

With deliberate slowness, Elizabeth rose. Though obligated to remain at the table, out of respect for her mother and for Mr. Hudson, she couldn't bear to trespass on the lovers' discussion one moment longer.

So much for a First Family Supper.

Four

Three days after her arrival in Mountain Home, Zylphia carried rugs into the back yard, hung them over the clothesline and beat them with vigor. She took tremendous satisfaction ridding her new home of dirt and dust. That Ina person might have thought herself a superior housekeeper—but she was not. Nor was she an outstanding cook.

Zylphia *would* prove her worth to her husband-to-be, one day's housekeeping after another, one well-prepared meal after another. Though he might not notice. Geo—such a *wonderful* man!—was far more interested in romancing her than in how clean his floors were.

She giggled, joy in her newfound circumstances lightening her spirits more than she'd believed possible.

The morning breeze carried puffs of dust

away. Birds twittered. And she'd not felt so alive in a long while.

If Geo hadn't left to deliver that large shipment of rifles to a mine—what had he called it? the Peerless?—he'd be with her still. But she was an industrious soul by nature. She wouldn't while away the afternoon. She had things to do before the family sat down to supper.

A baby laughed, drawing Zee's attention. Over the fence, a middle-aged woman tended to her flower and vegetable gardens. How lovely! A neighbor to become friends with.

Though she wore a dusty work dress and her hair was tied up beneath a scarf to keep out dirt and dust, she headed for the fence. The neighbor woman wasn't dressed better—how could she be? Tending to her garden, she wore a simple cotton dress meant for chores.

"Good morning." Zylphia leaned on the recently painted fence, offering a welcoming smile.

"Good morning to you." The woman had a hard time rising from her bent knees in the soil. She chuckled about her aching bones, and moved like a woman well into her fifties. No matter. What difference did age make? They could still be friends.

The neighbor, a good sixty to seventy pounds overweight, plump-cheeked and all smiles, picked up a baby from where it had lain on a quilt in the shade of a maple tree. "Who might you be?"

"Mrs. Zylphia Speare. I'll soon be Mrs. George Hudson."

"Oh, will you now?" The woman's reaction was filled with joy at the news. Such a relief, compared to that horrible Ina Dimond.

"I'm Babette Terrell. Call me Bab, won't you? My man is Archibald. Archie. Or just Arch."

"Call me Zylphia." She'd used her short name only with intimates. Just last night, she'd urged Geo to call her Zee. Maybe she and Bab would develop a close friendship and she'd invite Bab to use the nickname.

"Zylphia, it's a pleasure having you in the neighborhood. When is the wedding?"

"Soon."

The baby pumped his fat legs, wedged on either side of Bab's hip. The infant gnawed and slobbered on his own fist. The heat, such as it was, the little one was dressed only in a diaper and short dress. His bonnet kept away the worst of the sun. The perfect little cherub put her in mind of Elizabeth at that age. Such a happy baby.

"Meet my grandson. Archie, after his grandpa."

"A grandson—that's wonderful."

The perfect littler cherub reached for Zee but Bab pulled his wet fists back. "Oh, no you don't, Mr. Archie. Mrs. Speare doesn't want to hold the likes of you."

But she did. Very much. This fat and joyful baby, drooling all over his fist, was quite possibly the most beautiful little person she'd ever seen— other than her own.

For the first time, Zee wanted a grandchild. *There*, she'd admitted the truth to herself. *Want* seemed too mild to explain the ache in her breast. She *craved* a grandchild.

"May I?" She offered her arms, tentatively. Young Archie squealed with joy, pumped his chubby legs harder, and reached for Zee with welcome glee. Oh, how she *needed* a baby.

"He's wet."

"I don't mind." The little bundle, heavier than she'd anticipated, felt right in her arms. Right and absolutely wonderful. She cradled Archie close, and a flood of glorious memories rushed in and filled her eyes with tears.

She recalled the promise of holding her babies. Such dreams she'd had for them—and the familial bond that would keep them with her always. She'd been so alone before marriage and childbirth. Those babies were supposed to grow up and love her as she loved them.

She'd clung tightly to her sons, and those who'd lived had abandoned her, the thankless wretches. If it weren't for wonderful Geo, she might have grown old with no one but Elizabeth for company. Grateful, gentle Elizabeth. A good girl who understood her responsibilities as an only daughter.

"Have you grandchildren yet? Hope you don't mind me asking." Bab chuckled, as full of life and vitality as her grandson. "I saw your daughter out and about these past few days. A spitting image of you."

Zylphia nodded, forced the tears back.

"You do? How many?"

"Oh, no. No to the grandchildren question and yes about my daughter. Elizabeth Louise. My only daughter."

"Only one, you say? You and George have much in common."

Bab called Mr. Hudson by his first name? Worry caught Zee off guard, but as the neighbor chattered on, not a care in the world, she shook off the discomfort. Bab and Ina had *nothing* in common. This was the West. Colorado hadn't been granted statehood until nine years ago. Naturally, the unsettled places would be less observant of comportment than fine cities like St. Louis.

"Had only the one son, they did. Morgan's a fine young man. So much like his dad. I'm sure George will tell you all about it, wanting more children and all. He'll be a good grandpa, when the time is right."

If Elizabeth married, Zee would have a grandson or granddaughter of her own. But she couldn't bear the thought of a husband taking her precious daughter far away. No, that wouldn't do at all.

She knew all about men who picked up household and home and family and moved thousands of miles away without consulting his mother-in-law. She knew all about it—for she'd seen it time and time again. She must select a son-in-law with exquisite care.

If Elizabeth were to marry, he'd better be a man who'd keep her close. Like Morgan Hudson.

Geo said they had a close relationship. Morgan would stay home.

"I watched that boy grow up, follow his father to work through this very lot. Some days George couldn't get the boy to go to school, so enamored was he with the gunsmithing. Some days I think the pair of them have gun oil in their veins instead of blood."

"You like the Hudsons."

Bab chuckled. "Indeed, I do."

Elizabeth would do very well with Morgan Hudson. A perfect arrangement, really. A bond between George and herself. A grandchild that was *theirs*.

Moving matters along in that direction would take some thought. And a few nudges, but it could be done.

Baby Archie squealed with delight and patted Zee's face with his slobbery palm. Love for this child welled, filling her heart and overflowing. Well—she couldn't love this neighbor's baby, could she?

No, she just loved the idea of having another generation to love her back. A grandchild who'd live near, bring her happiness through her golden years, and see to her comfort as she grew old. A grandchild—several grandchildren—would ensure she was never alone.

"I see the men are living in the first house. That's good. And I've not seen Ina Dimond about since you arrived."

Zee's pleasure dimmed, a bucket of water thrown on the fire. "Why, yes, I dismissed Miss Dimond. I take great pleasure in keeping my own house and in feeding my own family. I'm not one to need hired help." Though she'd had plenty of domestics through the years. One did have to keep up appearances.

Bab didn't reply. The moment stretched, and Zee assessed her new friend's reaction. Had she overstepped? Had horrible Ina Dimond been a friend of Bab's? She swallowed. *Redirect. Redirect.* "I see how well you tend your gardens. You and I, I hope, are a good deal alike."

"Oh, yes, I think we are."

Relief swept in. Maybe, hopefully, Bab had been silent with her own thoughts.

"How old is Archie?" The babe's wet chin felt like heaven beneath her fingertip.

He grabbed her finger and chewed on it. Two little teeth had broken through the lower gum and by the feel of the upper, he'd soon have four pearly whites.

The simple touch reminded her of all she'd lost. Four babies, lost to illnesses in childhood. Buried in St. Louis. Their graves so far away, she'd never again visit. She'd lost her childbearing years. Old enough now, her marriage to Mr. Hudson would produce no issue.

All she had left was Elizabeth.

Wouldn't it be wonderful if Elizabeth married Morgan Hudson?

Five

By the time Mrs. Speare and her daughter had been in town one week, Morgan reassessed the situation. He'd known his relationship with Dad would change. He'd not been prepared for just how much.

Circumstances hadn't merely changed. They'd been shaken to the point Morgan was ready to hire a replacement for his father.

Other than helping load the wagon and delivering the rifles to Rocky Gideon at The Peerless Mine, Dad hadn't put in but a few hours here and a few hours there.

Orders were backing up.

Dad sat at his worktable and smiled, staring beyond the shaft of sunlight. The revolver he'd disassembled two days ago still sat in a neat row of individual components. This wasn't like Dad at all.

Unfortunately, Morgan couldn't live—or

work—with the man Mrs. Speare was turning Dad into.

He'd tried, the once or twice he'd crossed paths with his father's bride, to be civil. He couldn't comprehend what Dad saw in her.

Shoving aside the aggravation, he soaped and rinsed his hands at the washstand in the workroom. No sense bellyaching about circumstances he couldn't change.

Three more customers had brought in firearms for repair, and one had ordered a special piece. Put down a hefty deposit too.

At first, Morgan had gladly put in extra hours at the shop—the one place Mrs. Speare was sure to never be. He arose early and went to bed late. Hardly saw Dad, except when the old man sneaked back into the first house well after a proper hour.

Bells over the customer entrance jingled.

Perfect. Just *perfect*.

He couldn't man the counter and get anything done in back. He slapped on a smile, and left the workshop for the sales room out front.

"Ina." Now it wasn't hard to smile, seeing who'd come by. No sense staying behind the counter. He raised the pass-through section on its hinges and hurried to the woman who'd taken good care of his family.

Redness tinted her eyes and the tender tissues ringing them. She'd been crying but had done a fair job washing away the evidence.

Seeing her like this pained him. "I've been looking for you. Mrs. Speare—"

"I'm here about business."

Morgan pulled up short. "O.K.?"

Dear Ina wasn't as animated as that last night

in their home, but she wasn't her old, sweet self, either. "I want a gun."

He tried for jovial. "You've come to the right place."

"Something that shoots straight, every time. Something reliable."

Morgan had known real fear only once or twice in his life. One was the day he realized his mother was dying and he couldn't do one blasted thing about it. Now Ina scared him. *Bad*.

Did she intend to hurt herself?

"Are you in trouble?" If she needed help, he'd do anything for her.

"I—" She fidgeted, her movements shaky and too rapid. Her eyes darted left to right, left to right.

She wouldn't look at him. Instead, she paced the long, glass-faced counter top with pieces on display. And under lock and key.

'Bout now, that seemed more than prudent.

"Hey," he touched her elbow with the greatest of care. "It's *me*. Tell me what's wrong."

"I...I'm worried about intruders. I need to protect myself."

"From what?"

"From intruders." She repeated, but didn't seem to notice. "A break-in."

"Understandable." But no, it wasn't. "Something happen?" He regretted too-long hours and not enough time talking with friends and neighbors. If something had happened in town, he wouldn't know.

"I need a pistol. Something little I can carry in my pocket." She patted her hip.

Did women have pockets in their dresses? "We can manage that."

Uncertainty clawed at his gut. Grandpa had hammered responsibility into him—and so had Dad. Gunsmiths were duty-bound to sell *only* to those with sense.

"Ina." He touched her shoulder.

She flinched, whirled, and met his gaze for the briefest of moments, her eyes wild.

"You're not well. Tell me what's wrong."

The bells tinkled. *Again.*

Ina swung toward the door.

He wanted to push the customer out, bellow 'we're closed', and turn the key in the lock.

But it wasn't a customer. Just his waif of a soon-to-be stepsister in a plain, gray cotton work dress and apron. Her head uncovered. She'd obviously been working with her mother in the house.

Why did she always wear gray?

Arrah would never own clothes like that, much less wear them to town.

"Need something?" The question came out gruff and demanding.

Too late to stop her, Ina pushed past Elizabeth Speare, muttering plenty—and none of it complimentary toward Elizabeth's mother. Morgan couldn't blame her.

"Ina, wait." But she was out the door and up the street as fast as her feet could carry her.

Frustration and angst erupted. Morgan slapped his palm against the door frame. He couldn't go after her. Not without Dad in the shop. And securing the tools, revolvers, rifles, cash drawer, and securing dual locks on both the front and back doors took time. Time enough for Ina to be almost anywhere in town she wanted to go.

"I'm sorry."

Elizabeth would've bolted—he knew that—but he was too near the door and she wouldn't go through him. Nor would she flee out the back. She'd never been in the shop and the girl was too polite and too proper. "You're sorry."

"Yes. I'm sorry. I didn't realize your customer was Miss Dimond or I wouldn't have entered. The sunlight—my view through the window...I didn't recognize her."

He faced her fully then. She stood close. Too close. He would've thought she'd back up as far as the space allowed. "Need something?"

"Yes, I do."

The mouse stood up to him. Good for her.

"Ina Dimond is in love with your father."

What?

No. Ina looked after them because she'd been paid to...because she was a kind and generous-hearted woman without a family of her own.

And, in the end, they'd betrayed her.

That hadn't sat well with Morgan, not then and not now. He'd tried several times to find her at home, pay her the wages they owed with a substantial bonus, and apologize. But she'd been out.

Love? Ina loved Dad?

She'd been irrational upon learning supper guests were house guests, and house guests weren't actually guests at all, but soon-to-be-family...and smashed half the dishes in a fury.

"Close your mouth, Mr. Hudson."

He closed his mouth.

She tipped her head a little to the side. "Will she cause trouble for our parents, do you suppose?"

Our. Parents.

Most uncomfortable, that.

"Dad should have told her he'd proposed to your mother."

"Yes. And Mother should've shown an ounce of compassion."

Ah, so the little gray mouse not only stood up to him, she recognized her parent's shortcomings. His esteem rose a notch or two.

Maybe she wasn't like her shrew of a mother in more ways than one.

He didn't want to notice that, or anything else, about her, so he turned his focus to the street and Ina's distress.

"Does Ina have friends? Family? Women to talk to?"

"Uh—" Surely he knew, after all this time. "She's close with my aunt. Next-door neighbors."

"She needs a woman right now."

She smelled of roses. Elizabeth smelled of roses.

Three or four feet away, the roses in her bath soap tickled his nose.

He cleared his throat. Forced his wayward thoughts back to Ina. Somehow, letting Ina and Ray's mama, Aunt Maggie, talk it out, comfort each other, and speak ill of Mrs. Speare seemed a bit foolish. "You sure 'bout that?"

"I won't pretend to know Miss Dimond, but I know what it is to be a spinster."

"Spinster? You're what, nineteen? Twenty?"

"Didn't your mother teach you it's rude to ask a woman's age?"

"Can't say she did."

A shy, hesitant smile showed those beautiful teeth again.

"Why are your teeth perfect?" A stupid question, but she'd just called him on the last stupid question he'd asked. Maybe this one wasn't as offensive as her age.

"My father was a dentist."

"Ah."

"He insisted we take good care of our teeth."

Morgan shook his head, wondering about this woman who wouldn't tell him her age but freely talked of the father who'd died so recently. A dentist. No wonder his widow expected a house full of servants to keep things going. But that wasn't fair—Mrs. Speare had cooked three meals a day. Fed him every time he showed up, hoping to see Dad. Every time he'd not come to the new house for meals, she'd sent a plate to the shop or first house, usually with her daughter and occasionally with Dad. Neither stayed long enough for a conversation. Just handed him a plate.

She'd been nice, feeding him, even when he refused to be seated at her table.

Maybe he'd been too hard on the woman. Even if she had fired Ina.

He'd definitely been too hard on the woman's daughter. "Liz." He shook his head. "You're an enigma."

She chuckled, a warm, sweet sound he'd never heard. The girl was always so...*reserved.* "Everyone calls me Elizabeth Louise. Elizabeth for short."

"For short?" He snorted. "Elizabeth Louise. That's a mouthful."

"Maybe. My family doesn't use nicknames."

"Not even your brother?"

"Brothers. I have two, living."

Brothers.

For some reason he couldn't identify, he didn't like being lumped in with her journeyman carpenter brother in St. Louis. *He* wasn't her brother. Wouldn't be, not even when his father married her mother. If not siblings, then what were they?

"Junior is a merchant sailor."

That didn't make sense. "Isn't 'Junior' a nickname? And I thought he was a journeyman carpenter."

"Two brothers. Elijah Junior, after Father. Then Sidney, the carpenter. In St. Louis. I guess 'Junior' is a nickname."

"Junior *sails*. In St. Louis?"

And just like that, she smiled again, broad and genuine. He liked making her smile.

Somewhere along the way, she'd moved a little closer. She'd turned to the side, running her fingertips along the edge of the shelving. Not looking for dust. Just...exploring.

What did she want? He hadn't missed a meal, and she hadn't come delivering a plate. "You came out here for a reason?"

Her cheeks pinked. She seemed mighty interested in that shelf edge. "Not five minutes ago, a young gentleman came to the door, asking for me."

Morgan couldn't help it—he grimaced. "Who?"

"I don't know. Mother didn't give me a chance to ask."

Ray, probably. Wasn't one to wait on a good

thing. Ray looked mighty respectable in his suit of clothes. Had pretty manners too. Why would Mrs. Speare send him away?

"Mother said something you need to know about."

Oh boy. He could only imagine. "What's that?"

Her cheeks darkened to the color of rose petals. Probably just as soft. "Be forewarned. Mother said to that man, whoever he was, 'Elizabeth Louise intends to wed Morgan Hudson.'"

Six

His heart jumped into his throat. "*What?*"

She turned to him then, her expressive features pleading with him to believe her, to understand. "I couldn't have you thinking I'd come up with that idea. It was Mother—and Mother alone, I swear it."

Must she deny it with such vehemence? No matter what Arrah said, he wasn't a bad catch. He had a lot to offer a woman.

"I know," Liz insisted. "It's the oddest thing I've heard. You must understand, until yesterday morning, when another young man came to call—"

"Who?"

"Mr... I—I don't know."

"How many have come to the house?"

She lifted one slender shoulder in an uneasy shrug.

Who was he kidding? Liz was a lovely woman—if a bit young. Of course she'd have men coming to call, hoping to catch her attention, wanting to make her acquaintance. This ridiculous protectiveness arose from a sense of duty—and nothing more. The girl would be Dad's stepdaughter before long. Brothers were supposed to look out for their little sisters.

Completely normal.

Why was she so reticent? Had her mother uprooted her from St. Louis, forced Liz to leave a beau at home? It suddenly mattered, very much, that he knew. "Did you leave someone special in St. Louis?"

She laughed. A melodic, throaty melody that did strange things to his insides. "Me?"

"Yes, you. Why is that funny?"

"I've never had anyone special."

No suitors. No special fellow.

That made *no* sense. None whatsoever. A lovely young woman such as herself... "Unbelievable."

"Why?" *Now* she looked him full in the eye.

"I can't picture you alone."

"I've never had a beau." And the lack of male attention pained her. That much was obvious.

"You're a lovely young woman, Lizzy. I'm glad fellows around here have stopped by."

But he wasn't. Not glad at all.

Not *one* beau?

"Look—this isn't about me in St. Louis. This is about Mother's high-handed plan to push the two of us together. I've always known I wouldn't marry, that I'm not destined for that route, and now, with all of my school friends married for years and years, mothers of several children—"

"Whoa, whoa."

"Don't you see? That's my mother who told that young man I'm going to marry you. She's more aware than anyone I've never had a man's attention, never been courted."

"Back up. Further. What makes you think you're not destined for marriage?"

"I'm a spinster, Morgan Hudson. Passed over. On the shelf. An old maid." She sighed, but not in self-pity. The woman, evidently, had grown weary of repeating herself. "Mother's giddy in love with your dad, and somehow she came up with the idea that I should wed you, hence her disturbing statement to that young man at the door."

"I'm still stuck on her refusal to let him see you." Not that he wanted the unnamed swain to claim Lizzy's affections.

Dread settled in his gut. He didn't like where this was going. Not one bit.

She swallowed. The delicate movement of her throat drew his eye. "Mother's always been quick to tell me, as an only daughter, it's my responsibility to care for her, to remain with her as she grows older. She's been much worse in the months since my father's death."

That same rush of self-defense perked up its ears but he ignored it. For now. "Your mother holds onto you too tight. You're young, but I suspect you're of marriageable age."

"Ha. I'm twenty-six."

"You can't be twenty-six. Eighteen, maybe."

"Flattery, Mr. Hudson."

"Liz—call me Morgan. Mr. Hudson is my father."

She smiled, but sadly, and that weak ghost of a smile faded too quickly.

"Ignore your mother." He had. And the decision had been a good one.

"I've been torn, all week, between wanting to explain things to you so you'll understand, and trying to stay out of it."

That didn't sound like something he wanted to know.

"My mother is...difficult. When all is said and done, she can't bear to lose anyone else."

Widows often remarried long before they were ready. But that was the way of the world. Women needed financial support. Many had no choice.

"It's more than my father." Again, those blue eyes—so blue—pleaded with him to understand. "You heard Mother explain that Sidney remained in St. Louis with his work. That's true. What she didn't explain was that Sidney refused to accompany her. Outright refused."

Mrs. Speare had obviously messed up her children. "Sidney's older than you?"

"By two years."

"Twenty-eight?" Not that he believed Liz could be twenty-six, but for now, he'd play along. "Old enough to be on his own."

"Not in my mother's world. After Junior ran away to join the merchant sailors and never returned, then Father died suddenly..."

She held her breath, probably fighting tears. Who wouldn't shed a tear, so soon after a parent's death?

He gave her a minute, fighting the urge to touch her, merely to show kindness.

She waved a delicate, feminine hand, dismissing the pause in her explanation. "Mother grew up in an orphanage."

Oh. That had to color the way Zylphia saw the world, didn't it?

"She's overwrought, irrational with the fear of being alone."

Morgan didn't want to feel a spark of compassion for his stepmother-to-be. The woman could have been kidnapped by wild savages, sold into slavery aboard a whaling vessel, pressed into service aboard a pirate ship... And he didn't want to care.

But he remembered his own mama's kisses upon his cheeks when he'd grown tall enough he'd had to stoop to allow her to reach. Mama had been quick to express her love, along with urgency to take care. *Be careful, Son. You're my one and only.*

They would've filled the new house with offspring, if they'd been able. They'd wanted lots more. But in the end, no more came.

Mama had fretted over guns and emphasized safety. But she'd let him follow Dad into the business. She'd loved him enough to let him be his own man.

"My father," she whispered, "was shot in the street outside our home." Pain vibrated in her soft voice. "One morning on his way to the dental office. The police never caught the shooter."

What could he say to that? His mother's death was no one's fault, and had come at the end of a long, terrible road. They'd seen the Grim Reaper approaching, while yet a long way off.

Which was worse? Too much warning? Or not enough?

In the end, nothing anybody said had helped. He couldn't put his arms around this would-be sister, so he rested a hand on her shoulder. Just so she knew he was there. Just so she knew he cared.

"They say Dad was in the wrong place at the wrong time." She shook her head, disbelief pungent and acrid, like gunsmoke—unmistakable and unforgettable. "*Our* street. Daylight. *Right* place. *Right* time."

"When did this happen?"

"Six and a half months ago. Early December."

Scented, blue envelopes began arriving in January.

"I'm sorry." Empty words that offered no comfort. Empty words he'd hated for the years leading to Mama's passing and in the unbearable months and years afterward. "I'm sorry, Lizzy." He ached to pull her close, to hold her. In that moment, they were two people, more alike than he'd known and both grieving the loss of a parent. How could he not feel her pain?

She cleared her throat. "Rumor is Father had outstanding debts the business couldn't pay. His partner, another dentist, denied that rumor, but had no money to satisfy creditors. No money beyond the barest of necessities to see him properly buried."

Lizzy didn't need a discussion, she needed to talk, so he clamped his jaw.

This was why he'd become adamant that husbands and wives—or those headed to the altar—*needed* to talk about money. Men managing the money, without disclosing details to their wives, was a hopelessly old-fashioned and antiquated philosophy. Secrets served no purpose. How could a wife live within her husband's means if she had no information?

That argument had fed Arrah's discontent. In the end that argument had pushed her away—and probably saved them both a lifetime of discontent.

What had Mr. Speare kept from his wife? Anything? Nothing at all?

Morgan shook his head, even as he found himself rubbing Lizzy's shoulder. A caress—nothing less. He'd been pushing this girl, this *woman*, away. Because she had the gross misfortune of beauty, a strong resemblance to Arrah, and the calamity of birth to Zylphia Speare.

No more.

The absurd treatment of this tenderhearted girl would cease. Instantly. Next time she brought him a meal, he'd thank her. He'd look her in the eye. He'd treat her like the compassionate lady she was.

"So." She let out a huge breath of air. "Now, perhaps, you understand my mother. And won't be too hard on her as her machinations play out."

Oh, yeah. Mrs. Speare's newfound determination to see him wed to her daughter.

Number one problem with that? He couldn't abide anybody telling him what to do. Zylphia suggested it, therefore he couldn't. That simple.

But this was Lizzy...

"Lizzy—you do realize it's ridiculous to buy into your mother's neediness. You're a grown woman. It's not your job to tend her, to make sure she's not alone. She has my dad now."

"I told you all of that so you'd see—it *is* my responsibility, as an only daughter, to remain with my mother."

That rubbed Morgan the wrong way, fingernails on a chalkboard. "I don't need to ask where you found that fool idea."

She shrugged off his hand, rejecting more than his touch. She'd rejected him and everything he'd just said.

"Ridiculous? You followed your father—did what he wanted you to, when he taught you gunsmithing. Why is this different?"

"Gunsmithing is an honorable way for a man to make a living. It's honorable to follow a father, to learn his work." Her brothers hadn't followed their dad into dentistry, so she didn't understand.

She raised one brow as if to ask, "And?"

"Do you think for yourself?" he challenged.

Anger sparked in the blue of her eyes. "Oh, yes. More than you'd suppose."

"What are you going to do about your meddling mother?"

"I'm going to let her think she's succeeding. That we're doing what she suggests. It's easiest. Less messy."

"Let her think she's succeeding? I need you to spell that one out for me—are we talking wedding plans?" He didn't think he could do that—his wounds had only recently scabbed over. He couldn't convincingly playact.

"I'll work here with you. In the shop. I can wait on customers, even if I can't repair a revolver."

He didn't like the sound of that. Not at all.

"We can be companionable at supper. Smile at one another, can't we?"

That meant he'd have to sit at the dining room table nightly and watch Dad, the lovesick swain. "Well, yes, but—"

"Our parents are giddy in love. I walked into the kitchen and caught them kissing." She blanched. "No peck on the cheek." She wouldn't meet his gaze, but stood a little taller. Chalk up one more tally in the *Respect for Lizzy* column.

"They want privacy."

"Not a good idea."

"Have *you* had the incomparable pleasure of walking in on them?" She groaned and covered her eyes. "They're going to carry on, whether I'm in the house or not. I have no desire to be an unwilling audience. Seven months ago, Mother was kissing my father. I remember them embracing on Thanksgiving Day. I might be the only one who thinks it's too soon. Have you any idea how difficult it is for me to see her in your father's arms?"

That struck home. He cleared his throat and discarded the argument. "You want to come to work here, in the shop, avoid another embarrassing experience. That I can understand."

"I don't want to chaperone our parents."

He'd have a talk with his father, just as soon as he came in to bed that night—no matter how late. A talk he was so not looking forward to. But if Liz didn't want to talk to her mother, he couldn't make her.

"Listen to me." She stood her ground. One more tally mark in the *Respect* column. "I won't chaperone my mother. That's like poking a rattlesnake. She's a grown woman and she's in love with your father. I also know she's decent and has high expectations for proper behavior."

"All right."

"Back to her statement to that young man,

whoever he was. That statement that I've chosen you and we'll soon be married? Trust me—I know my mother. The *only* way to keep her off our backs is to ensure she believes we're headed in that direction."

"Toward marriage."

"Yes." She scowled. "The world is not coming to an end, Mr. Hudson."

"My name's Morgan. Your mama won't believe we're headed anywhere together if you call me Mr. Morgan in her hearing."

"Ugh." She sighed, folded her arms, and held his gaze far longer than he found comfortable. "If we're keeping company—or at least Mother *believes* we are—she'll sit back and let nature take its course. She won't be harping on it day and night. Won't dream up ways to force us together."

Doing what Zylphia wanted rubbed him the wrong way. "I don't have to kiss you, hold your hand, dote on your every word?" In short, he didn't have to act like Dad.

If he were fool enough to act like a man in love, it wouldn't be long until those dubious scabs sloughed off...

Not a good idea, tempting fate like that.

"No, you do not need to kiss me or hold my hand. This is a *ploy*, Morgan. To make Mother see what isn't there. Would it kill you to *almost* dote on my every word?"

He glimpsed pain in her eyes in the second before she looked away. This poor girl hadn't ever known a fellow's attention. No courtships, no gentleman callers. He couldn't blame her for wanting a scrap of affection.

He'd been a fool, an idiot—and unkind. Lizzy

deserved better. *So* much better. Hadn't he vowed to stop treating her badly?

"Will you come in for supper?" Her self-assurance was riddled with holes. Holes he'd punched out, one at a time.

"Yes. I'll be at the supper table."

For her, he'd come back to that dining room table.

For her, he'd welcome her at the shop, put her to work, find something for her to do...and give up his last safe haven.

For her, he'd brave the company of an old couple so in love they forgot their manners and reminded Morgan what it was like to love a woman.

Five minutes with Dad, in the old man's close association with Zylphia, and Morgan's thoughts would center on kissing Lizzy.

Her smile, wide and bright and genuine, shone with the heat of the noonday sun.

He was in *so* much trouble.

Seven

After one week of working in the gunsmith shop with Morgan, Elizabeth found she'd become quite comfortable with the work. She could write up a work order, sell cartridges, and assist customers who returned to pick up their repaired pistols and rifles.

The only challenge to the new routine was keeping a tight rein on her feelings for Morgan...and handling the increase in traffic through the door.

At least Morgan said the day-to-day customers had doubled. Why that made him cranky, she couldn't understand.

She couldn't repair or build custom orders, but she waited on patrons and the predominately male patrons liked her. Astonishing, really, as at first, she couldn't distinguish a .45 Colt

Peacemaker from a .36 Remington Single Action Revolver.

Early in the afternoon of July first, she neatly wrapped Mr. Dahl's purchase. "Enjoy your day, Mr. Dahl."

"You've made my day a happy one already, Miss Speare."

"Good-bye now." Elizabeth waved as the elderly man leaned heavily on his cane and with fifty tiny steps, made his way through the door. The bells jingled.

"You're not like her." Morgan leaned on the door frame where the workshop and sales floor adjoined. Morgan had apparently been watching. He did that a lot. No doubt to ensure she handled his customers with kindness. She'd explained that the shop's success was in her own best interest; the shop supported the Hudsons—and the Hudsons fed and housed her.

"I'm not like who? Mother?"

He pushed off the frame and approached. He leaned an elbow on the counter. So near, his heat warmed the space between them. "Yes. You're not like her. I rather like you."

She laughed.

He made her laugh, often.

He grinned like a silly fool. A dear, amazing, *wonderful* fool.

"I rather like you too." And that's where it had to stop. After all, they playacted affection, and pretended courtship. So far, Mother had been blissfully happy and quite clueless about their hoax. Besides, Mother wasn't in the shop to benefit from the show.

"Good." His voice lowered in volume and

pitch. "We like each other."

Heat crept up her cheeks. She busied herself tidying the counter, brushing the odd scraps of twine she'd trimmed from the ends of Mr. Dahl's package, and dropped them into the waste basket.

"You're blushing." He bumped her with his shoulder.

"I am?"

"Don't fret. It's adorable."

Heat surged higher. Now her ears would be red.

"You're adorable."

Why must he delight in making her blush? She'd prefer he make her laugh. "Don't you have work to do?"

"I finished the rifles Murphy brought in."

"Oh, the grocer. Good. He came in earlier, asking about them."

"I heard."

That was the problem. Morgan heard *everything* that happened out front. Much of his work didn't make enough noise to cover the conversation after conversation. As if he stood at her side, all day long.

He leaned nearer yet. His breath teased the fine hairs at her temple. "Your ears are pink, Lizzy Lou."

"That's quite enough, Morgan."

He chuckled.

Time to change the subject. "I've been wondering about something."

"What's that?"

"How long has your mother been gone?"

The teasing light in his eyes faded. "Three years."

She nodded, containing a rush of compassion for his sadness. Each time he'd spoken of his mother, his love for her had been evident—a sharp contrast to her brothers. Junior and Sidney admitted or showed affection for Mother, but only under duress. They'd taken after Father, preferring to shun love. If either brother had an ounce of affection for Elizabeth, they'd never demonstrated it.

Given the contrast, how could she *not* admire Morgan's uncommon capacity?

He had a big heart. And had no need to bury his feelings. She loved that about him.

"What happened?"

He didn't answer right away, so she intentionally allowed him time to find his words.

"Cancer. In her belly." Seconds ticked past on the wall clock. His gaze focused on the past, in that far-away place.

"She was ill for two years."

He fell silent. How awful, to watch a parent's health fail, and be unable to help. She understood comfort measures—cold compresses, reading aloud, sitting nearby for hours on end...

But to watch his mother slowly dying must've been unbearable.

"I'm sorry." She took a risk and touched him. The simple gesture of her hand upon his back, when she wanted to embrace him...

Not a good idea.

"People are born." His voice, rough and thick, betrayed his pain. "Some die young. Some grow old."

"You loved her. You *love* her still."

"Yes."

He remained lost in his thoughts a moment more while she swept a palm over his back and admired his sturdy, muscled form. So masculine. So...*big*. Another circling motion, allowing fingernails to lightly abrade.

Looking had been one thing—but to touch was altogether *more*.

She forced herself to be still, to let her hand upon his back express comfort, and *only* comfort.

She cleared her throat. "Were you close? Your mother and you?"

"Mama said I was her whole life." He chuckled in a way that seemed sad. "When I was small, I thought I understood. Now I see she loved my dad with her entire heart, with her whole heart left for me."

He met her gaze then, held it in a way that seemed shockingly intimate. "Love for spouse and love for son are two different capacities."

What was he trying to say?

"Yes." She caught herself, her thumb tracing a ridge of muscle. An amazing physique—one more thing to love about him. "I see your parents must have been happy."

"You sound wistful." He watched her closely. "Your parents were unhappy?"

Admitting the truth about her parents' marriage seemed untrue to Father's memory...but this was Morgan. In a matter of days, her mother would be his mother too. He deserved to know, because, like her childhood in the orphanage, she was a result of her experiences...and marriage to Father made her who she was. Understanding Mother would make their relationship easier.

"I'll answer my question first." He smiled

softly. "My parents were blissfully happy."

"You know this, how?"

"We lived in that one-room house. Can't hide a spat from your child during long winters or a solid week of rain."

She laughed.

"I think that's why Dad wants to remarry. To him, marriage means happiness." He turned his whole body toward her. He caught the hand she'd placed upon his back, and held it between his.

Her insides tingled. He held her hand the way courting couples held hands…and it felt *wonderful*. She looked up from their joined hands and witnessed a twinkle in his eyes.

And fell a little more in love.

She was in *so* much trouble.

"I'll admit, Lizzy Lou, I was scared for Dad the day we met you at the train and your mother disembarked in that horrible, *horrible* purple gown."

She laughed. "I told her not to wear it but she insisted. Meeting your father for the first time had her in a fit of nerves. She changed in the ladies' room while I tended the naughty Gideon boys. "

"Tell me she does not intend to wear that *best dress* at the wedding. If so, it needs to disappear."

She chuckled at his antics. This loving, big-hearted man, had learned from the best possible example. "Your dad has made my mother happier than she's ever been. I can admit that, to you." She focused on their joined hands again, and soaked up the beautiful closeness this simple touch invoked.

"I like that."

Her pulse quickened. His thumb swept over hers. She closed her free hand, opened it, aching to touch him, to at least settle that empty hand upon his forearm. Twenty-six, and she didn't know how to hold hands.

"Your parents weren't happy?" He genuinely wanted to know.

"Not like yours. It's heartbreaking how desperately Mother loved him—he meant everything," She winced. "That didn't come out right...She *loves* your dad."

His smile warmed her clear to her toes. "I know. I see their happiness. I never thought it possible—after that purple gown—but their love is undeniable."

"Yes."

"Dad's only fifty. He might live another year or thirty. He *deserves* the happiness he found with your mother."

How could she not love this man? Smiling broadly, she glanced down, then back into his eyes.

"I apologize," he murmured, "for thinking poorly of your mother at first."

"The purple dress was quite horrid."

He laughed. "Not what I meant, but you're kind to let me off the hook."

She nodded, and noted she'd somehow moved a step nearer, so drawn to Morgan Hudson. Just like Mother, who felt that same tremendous pull toward George Hudson.

Mother and daughter. Drawn to father and son.

This had to be the oddest circumstance ever. She'd never thought, not for a moment...

If she married Morgan, their children—if they had children—would have *one* set of grandparents. That sounded...*wrong*.

But her hand in Morgan's, dallying during the workday while he had an enormous list of work to accomplish felt *incredibly right.*

He felt incredibly right.

What would it be like to have a man as in love, as committed, as George Hudson for Mother?

As demonstrated with his first wife, Morgan's mother, George knew how to love a woman without restriction or limitations. *So* unlike her own father. The more tightly Mother had clung, desperate for affection, the more Father had pulled away, suffocated and unhappy.

Morgan Hudson would love without limits, like his father. "What was your mother's name?"

"Matilda Morgan. Everyone called her Tildie."

She smiled—with him, smiling was easy. "I see."

"Indeed you do. Mother's maiden name became my Christian name. My parents' choice pleased my Grandfather Morgan. Ten daughters, and no one to carry on the name."

Voices sounded on the boardwalk outside the shop, the doorbell tinkled, and a man entered.

That quick, the tender closeness between them ended. Morgan stepped away and opened the ledger upon the counter as if he'd been reaching for the book when the customer entered.

"Ray." Morgan sounded pleased to see his cousin. The Hudsons had mentioned Raymond and the Cresswell family as they'd discussed the wedding over supper each evening.

"Hey, Morgan." The cousin removed his hat, revealing thick hair a shade or two darker than Morgan's. His tidy suit of clothes, snowy white collar , and precisely knotted necktie told her plenty about him. He bowed in an easy manner, gallant yet flirty. "Good afternoon, Miss Speare."

She glanced to Morgan—then back. "Mr. Cresswell."

"Ah! They *have* mentioned me. Raymond Cresswell, at your service." Anyone else would've sounded absurd, but Morgan's cousin charmed. Probably had a dozen ladies swooning and one hundred close friends.

"A pleasure, sir. May I help you?"

"Actually, yes." Ray flipped his hat over his forearm in a flashy move, reached across the counter, bold as could be, and grabbed her clasped hands. "Morgan, be a pal and give us a moment alone, will you?" According to Morgan, Ray had been one of the fellows who'd come to the house to see her. "I want to talk to the lady alone."

"She's working." Morgan read through yesterday's page in the sales ledger, as if searching for something.

"You have time for me, don't you, Miss Speare?"

"I'm busy." She tugged but Ray refused to let her go.

He laughed—so unlike Morgan, self-gratifying...with an edge. "No one in the store but me, pretty lady."

She'd had essentially no experience with men. No man, decent or otherwise, had ever flirted with her. Society frowned on public flirtations so she'd witnessed very little. But this...*excess*...made her uncomfortable.

She pulled again and this time his grip loosened. She eased back from the counter.

His smile faded, and deviousness in his eye

gave her pause. Her heart pounded, and she found herself relieved Morgan hadn't left the sales room. With him at her side, she felt safe, if not harassed.

"I came to my Aunt Tildie's house, hoping to make your acquaintance," Mr. Cresswell said, his voice carefully even. "But your mother wouldn't allow me to see you."

He observed her, his features hard. She didn't dare glance to Morgan. "My mother is strict, Mr. Cresswell. And fastidious."

He shook his head. "I think you refused to see me."

Perhaps her mother was more discerning and less selfish than Elizabeth had believed.

Did he enjoy making her feel like a cornered mouse, and he, the cat who batted a paw. No wonder young women refused to see him.

"Actually, I had no idea you'd come to the door."

"Well, I'm here now. Don't you want to know why I called?"

She waited, taking clues from Morgan. What would Ray do next?

"I will accompany you about town on Independence Day. Big day of entertainment, all kinds of distractions."

She knew all about the festivities planned. Four men had already extended invitations, working up to it by sharing the details. Each were kind, genteel, and gracious upon hearing she'd promised to accompany Mother and Mr. Hudson.

"I've promised my mother and her intended, Mr. Hudson, I'd accompany them on Independence Day."

"Is that so." A statement, rather than

question. All pretense of good humor had fled.

"Yes. Mr. Hudson wishes to introduce Mother and me to neighbors and friends."

"Uh-*huh*."

"You *are* aware my mother and Mr. Hudson are to be married?"

"I'd heard." The dapper gentleman who'd entered the shop tarnished further with every sentence spoken, peeling paint, revealing the ghoul beneath.

"Your stepdaddy is my uncle." Cresswell leaned on the glass-fronted display case, then shot Morgan a superiority-soaked glance. "I'll join your party. Uncle George welcomes me."

The more Ray Cresswell said, the less she liked him. "Thank you, Mr. Cresswell—"

"I will arrive at eight."

"Actually, Mr. Cresswell—"

"Can't miss the pancake breakfast. Important flag-raising ceremony."

"No." She held her ground. "Thank you, but no."

"You're not patriotic, Miss Speare?" He *tsk-tsk*ed. "No patriotism. What will people say?"

"*Good day*, Mr. Cresswell." She nodded at the door.

"That's not nice, Miss Speare."

She'd come to the end of her rope. "*Good-bye.*"

"I've made plans—told the fellas—"

"As have I. Made plans, that is. *Good day.*" She could leave. Shut the door and hide in the workroom until Morgan saw his cousin out. But somehow that wouldn't be nearly as satisfactory as finishing this herself.

Cresswell reached across the counter, a swift strike, and made a grab for her.

He put her in mind of a king-sized rattler.

He nearly caught her.

She backed up, just in time, and Morgan, who'd been leafing through the book seemingly without a care in the world, clutched his cousin's wrist. A manacle locked tight.

Her heart pounded, hard. She fought to stifle a squeak, gasp, or any sign that he'd frightened her. Men like him thrived on power.

Morgan and Ray challenged one another without a word passing between them. Her heart pounded, and as she watched, her confidence in Morgan doubled. He knew when to fight, and how. He defended her, despite the fact the other man was his cousin and friend.

After a charged moment, Morgan released Ray, who stepped back and subtly rubbed his wrist. With a practiced move, he rolled his hat onto his head at a cavalier angle.

"I'm surprised, Miss Speare. Thought I'd find a lady when I met you." He shook his head, implying she were anything but.

Elizabeth raised her chin. She would not be easily cowed, nor would she grant him power over her. "You are not welcome here, Mr. Cresswell. Show yourself out."

"Not welcome in my uncle's shop?" He shook his head with over-dramatized disbelief. "I believe it is you who is unwelcome, Miss Speare."

Morgan shut the book, and with an ease she hadn't anticipated, took her in his arms. Easy, at home, simple, convincing. He held her with the grace and comfort of a man who'd done all of those things frequently and forever. He kissed her temple, his warm lips lingering at her hairline for the longest of moments.

She couldn't help it. Her eyes drifted shut with a combination of relief and an overwhelming joy.

This was precisely what she wanted. *Morgan*.

"You're too late," Morgan told his beast of a cousin. "The *lady* has chosen me."

"Your *sister*, you fool." Cresswell tugged on his lapels, straightening his coat as if girding himself for battle. "Always were cracked."

Morgan's embrace tightened, but not in anger, not in an attempt to restrain his temper. He tightened his arms about her and it felt like...like *love*.

Genuine. Motivated by heartfelt affection. The natural manifestation of a man for a woman he'd promised his life to.

Tears threatened—but she would not, *could not*, allow Raymond Cresswell to think he'd won.

The tears of joy, tears...because her soul recognized in this man, Morgan Hudson, the completion she'd thought would never come. Not for her.

The man she loved had taken her in his arms and claimed her.

She'd have to be dead inside to not shed a tear of joy, wouldn't she?

Morgan chuckled, soft and low, sounding so much like Mr. Hudson as he hugged Mother close in a stolen embrace when they believed themselves alone. "No, Ray," Morgan repeated. "I meant *precisely* what I said. You are too late. The lady is *mine*."

Morgan's declaration, resonating with conviction, was finally the impetus to carry Ray Cresswell over the threshold. Ray strode down the street in long, brisk strides.

And still, Morgan lingered, his lips pressed to her temple, his arms about her.

Despite the thunder and lightning of Ray's temper, a visceral reaction tore through Elizabeth's middle. Hope flared, a flash of light to accompany the electrical storm. She was as stunned as if she'd been struck by that bolt of lightning herself, or as if the thunder had boomed directly overhead.

Oh, no.

She didn't like this. Not any of it. Not the threat Ray Cresswell posed. Not the flash of desire rooted in her heart. Not the vows Morgan had been forced to make.

Bereft, empty, and shaking, she reminded herself it wasn't real.

The courtship wasn't true.

She wasn't really his lady.

She'd vowed she would not allow their playacting to confuse her heart.

Before, when she'd had control over her heart and affections. She'd remembered the cost to her sanity if she'd lost control, if she'd fallen in love. Because of who she was, because of the weird situation with their parents, she was last on his list. Even now, Morgan, in his uncommon decency, had pretended to ensure her safety. He'd put himself between her and his crude cousin, to ensure, for the time being, the idiot left her alone.

She trembled against him, chilled to the bone, despite the heat of the day.

Unfailingly kind, Morgan held her tighter. He

nudged her to turn more fully into him and settled her against his heart. He cradled her. Gently. No rush. No demands. No orders.

A perfect rendition of exactly what she wanted. Everything she'd always wanted and believed she'd never find.

And turned her into himself, cradled her with gentleness and a glimmer of all she desperately wanted. With him.

If *only* this man could love her.

Anguish, full-bodied and horrible to behold washed through her—a flash flood on the heels of that lightning storm.

She'd become her mother.

The woman who loved Elijah Speare, loved him irrationally, far better than Elijah could love her in return. Love had pushed him away, to the brink and farther still—until Mother remained in that marriage alone.

Loving him completely, and needing far more than he could give.

Still, Morgan rocked her. Back and forth. He kissed her forehead. "He's gone."

She nodded. Tears streamed down her face.

Where would they go from here?

Somehow, he pulled his handkerchief from his pocket and pressed it into her hand, yet never released her.

Eventually, her tears eased and her breathing become even.

Morgan stilled as she calmed. He held her against his chest, his breaths slowing, the lullaby of his heartbeats reassuring.

He felt good, right. She'd utterly, completely, lost her heart to him.

"Lizzy Lou," he whispered, "I can't think of you as a sister. I never could."

She nodded, though she didn't quite believe him. He might *think* so, but their definitions would be different. *So* different.

"You're going to the Independence Day Celebration with me."

She nodded, clinging tightly, knowing this precious moment in his arms drew to a close.

"You're safe with me, Lizzy."

She nodded.

"Do you understand?"

He sought her face, no doubt mottled with splotches and puffiness and insecurities.

He walked her through the door into the back room, sat her in a chair well out of sight from the front door, and brought her a glass of water.

She drank, though she didn't really want it. All she wanted was to remain in his arms forever.

"Give me thirty minutes. I'll clean up, lock up, and I'll walk you home."

Eight

On the morning of Independence Day, Elizabeth accepted Mother's invitation to prepare, together, for the day's events. Two windows stood open, the screens keeping out insects but allowing cross-ventilation. The morning remained gloriously cool in this high mountain valley. Not nearly as hot or humid as St. Louis, the day would be warm but so enjoyable.

Mother took her turn at the dressing table. With care, Elizabeth lifted the hot curling iron from its lamp, and applied it to Mother's bangs.

"I'm so pleased." Mother fairly bubbled over with happiness. "You and Morgan. *Perfect.* You two make the most handsome couple."

Elizabeth's stomach turned a somersault. "Thank you, Mother."

If only it weren't playacting...and a soon-to-be

stepbrother's kindness. She'd replayed his actions, defending her from Raymond Cresswell, over and over again—and Morgan's words.

He'd been so sincere—so affectionate. Could she trust herself to know the difference?

Mother had complimented and carried on, whispering and planning, joyfully, since Elizabeth had shared the news of Morgan's invitation.

"You do look captivating in that dress, Elizabeth Louise, even if it hasn't a proper bustle. The color flatters the blue of your eyes."

"Thank you."

The freshly ironed blue gingham reflected in the dressing table's mirror as she applied the curling iron to yet another lock of Mother's hair.

"Why haven't you worn it before today?"

She'd been able to accept the bright blue of the gingham dress, only because of its simple lines and timeless form. Even without the high fashion, the dress made her uncomfortable. How could she explain that to a woman who knew no such feelings? Plain gray didn't put her on display, didn't catch the eye, didn't make a spectacle...as if she tried too hard to fancy up her plain face.

She had no delusions of beauty. If only she'd favored her mother more than her father.

But all the wishing in the world wouldn't make it so.

"I saved it for this special occasion." A much easier answer. What occasion could be better?

Morgan had invited her to accompany him under duress, true, but she would ensure this social outing was enjoyable. For him as well as herself.

Memories of his chaste kisses, his embrace, his whispered *I can't think of you as a sister, Lizzy*

Lou. I never could.

And she hadn't been able to think of him as a brother.

Her belly tingled with anticipation. Where did that leave them?

Mother tittered on and on. So much happier than Elizabeth had seen her in a very long while.

"Tell me." Mother's eyes sparkled with shared secrets. "I want to know how you and Morgan are coming along."

Elizabeth held a curl in place while it cooled, and set the iron back on its heating lamp. "Quite well."

"But do you *like* him?"

Since when had Mother ever wanted to know if she was fond of a man?

"I do. Very much. He's a good man."

"Just like his father, don't you think?"

"I do."

"I think it's *marvelous* that you and Morgan are attending the festivities together. And even better that you're courting. Just think what it could be like, Elizabeth. The four of us. Happily entwined into one happy family."

When Mother put it that way, it seemed almost...*possible.*

"I told Geo that you two should marry."

She couldn't admit entertaining the same wishes, in the most secret recesses in her heart. "Oh?"

"As husband and wife, you and Morgan should live in this big house with us. Soon it'll be too cold in that drafty cabin."

"That would be lovely, wouldn't it?" She'd not been able to suppress the daydreams. But her daydreams always centered on her and Morgan in that lovely, snug cabin. The two of them, quiet and building a life together, just the two of them. Let their parents live in the big house.

Mother held a gold eardrop to her right ear, a pearl to the left, assessing her reflection. "And Geo believes it's a fine idea. The four of us, here, together. It's precisely what he wants to see happen. Having only one son gives him the best understanding—he understands why I'm so careful with you."

Mother met Elizabeth's gaze in the mirror, obviously awaiting a reply.

"Yes."

"So, now that we've settled on Sunday for our nuptials, and the plans are in motion, the only thing that remains is seeing you properly dressed, Elizabeth Louise."

No sense arguing, though her nicest of plain, gray dresses would do. This occasion wasn't about her, and she had no interest in attracting attention. "We haven't time to engage a seamstress, nor have a gown made. Even if we did, you're the bride. You need a dress."

"I have something. I'm prepared. You wouldn't think I'd wait until mere days before my wedding to consider a gown, do you?"

In St. Louis, Mother had kept standing weekly appointments with the dressmaker. She'd enjoyed spending Father's money—perhaps a little too much. "No, Mother."

"Something cool in this heat. But not white. And not gray." Mother smoothed her pale blue summer dress, the finest piece she brought with her from home. Far nicer than the purple monstrosity. She couldn't help but smile, remembering Morgan's reaction.

"You're smiling." Mother turned on the stool to look Elizabeth in the eye. "What is it? Tell me."

Criticism of Mother's purple silk costume would not please her. "Anticipating your wedding day. You'll make a lovely bride."

Joy erupted over Mother's features, and she seemed so young and buoyant, as if the weight and misery of last winter and Father's loss had never occurred.

She had Mr. George Hudson to thank.

"You'll be every bit as happy, my dear." Mother spun back to face the mirror, apparently settling on the gold eardrops. She fastened one to her left earlobe. "You'll see. Any day now, your charming Morgan will declare himself and then we will be planning your marriage."

Elizabeth wasn't so certain. She might dream, but she didn't dare hope. She'd not been passed over all these years without cause. To assume matters would change now, simply because Morgan Hudson had come into her life, seemed presumptuous.

Mother donned her right earring, turned a little to the left, then to the right, admiring her appearance. With only a few white hairs, and retaining the slender figure of her youth, Mother remained a beauty. She'd taken great pains to avoid the sun on her hands and face, making use of gloves and parasol every time she went out.

"You're beautiful, Mother."

"Thank you, my darling daughter. Thank you." Mother's focus was upon her reflection, and, as typical, didn't think to examine Elizabeth once more and return the favor. Even if Elizabeth were no great beauty.

How could she, untried, inexperienced, and hopeless, think to hold Morgan's attention?

Nine

Mountain Home's Independence Day Celebration was far grander than Elizabeth had anticipated. People must have come from ranches and little communities surrounding the town, for the streets and public places were more crowded than Elizabeth had ever seen.

True to his word, Morgan had escorted her from event to event, urging her to choose which of the offerings appealed to her the most. His only commitment was hosting the shooting competition, a tradition officiated by the Hudsons since the first Independence Day event in Mountain Home.

Morgan had seated Elizabeth on a park bench in the shade to rest, an hour before the event. Not five minutes before, Mother and Mr. Hudson had kept her company, but Mother had flitted off, dragging Mr. Hudson along.

Elizabeth suspected George Hudson should've been helping set up the targets against a densely packed barrier of hay, not attending to Mother. But Morgan had things under control.

She noticed familiar faces entering the park. She stood and waved to catch her friend's notice. "Felicity! Mrs. Gideon!"

The handsome couple and their two boys—remarkably better behaved with their father on hand—were all smiles and handshakes.

"May I introduce my husband, Mr. Rocky Gideon, owner of The Peerless *and* these two rascals."

Elizabeth laughed at Felicity's buoyant good humor. This couple's love for each other and for their young children was obvious in every movement, touch, and word. Often, Elizabeth had been able to convince herself she was better off a spinster. But not when faced with Rocky and Felicity Gideon.

"It's so good to see you again." Felicity held onto the two-year-old, fighting to keep him in her arms. His brother perched on his father's shoulders, far better behaved than on the train.

"And you." Mrs. Gideon had invited her to come by their home, a big house on the fringes of town. So much time had elapsed—and she'd not paid a call. "I'm working at the gunsmith shop. Mr. Hudson's so busy with entertaining Mother, he's not...working much."

Felicity laughed in good humor. "The wedding is soon?"

"Yes. It seems every conversation is about the details."

"Targets!" The elder son yelled from his perch on Mr. Gideon's shoulders. "They's gonna shoot targets." He made a little-boy sound reminiscent of a firing pistol. "I shoot guns!" Little fingers playacted steps of aiming with one eye closed, pulling the trigger, and blowing gunsmoke from the barrel.

"You do?" Elizabeth wiggled the boy's shoe and smiled at him.

The boy chattered on, happily, gesturing with both arms and a toothy grin.

His father held on tight to his son's ankles, lest he tumble off.

"I think lots of people want to watch the contest." Elizabeth had lost her seat on the bench to an elderly couple. The street had filled, more and more people headed toward the contest arena. Ropes strung from sawhorse to sawhorse kept observers at a distance.

"Daddy shoot good?" The boy patted his father's head. "You win?"

"I might." Rocky Gideon wore a holster about his belt, his pistols likely a temptation to eager fingers. No wonder he'd put the boy upon his shoulders and out of reach. "I'd best sign in." He kissed his wife's cheek. "Coming?"

"I'm sorry, Elizabeth—Do stop by, won't you? First chance?"

"I will. I promise."

The Gideons made their way through the crowd, and Elizabeth decided to follow. She caught a glimpse of a familiar face beneath one of a hundred bowler hats. But that *couldn't* be...

She paused, watched through the crowd of milling people—and sure enough, the man in question—slender, not remarkably tall, brown hair and brown eyes, fastidious in dress, had just tucked his watch back into his pocket.

Her heart rate spiked. Adrenaline flooded her system.

Wardie Ferwinckle! What on earth was Wardie doing in Mountain Home? The young man had been Father's partner, fresh from dental school. The last she'd seen him had been at the funeral services—*months* ago.

He ambled through the pressing crowd and Elizabeth lost sight of him—one more brown suit of clothes and one more brown bowler in a sea of men in their finery.

Obvious one moment—invisible the next. She swallowed, her throat dry. Her pulse continued to pound.

Morgan—*she needed to tell Morgan.*

"Miss Speare?"

Above the din, a man's voice, familiar. She spun to him.

Ray Cresswell. The *last* thing she wanted was a conversation without Morgan present.

He removed his hat, without flourish, without peacocking. "Ma'am."

"Mr. Cresswell." She nodded and put a quick end to the exchange. Despite the crowd and public street, she wasn't comfortable.

"I mean you no harm, Miss Speare. I want to apologize."

The fool seemed genuine, sincere. Good manners warred with her desire to leave. *Where* was Morgan?

Had he left the targets for the sign-in table?

The most unsettling sensation of being

watched prickled at her skin.

Mr. Ferwinckle? Did Father's dental partner lurk in the growing crowd, watching her, waiting for a vulnerable moment to strike?

"I behaved poorly in the shop when I saw you last." Ray shifted with discomfort. "I apologize, Miss Speare and beg your forgiveness. I was not myself that afternoon."

Did she dare ask Mr. Cresswell to escort her to Morgan's side? It seemed Raymond Cresswell's ill behavior had been exacerbated by his cousin's presence. Like two dogs with one bone, the cousins hadn't been courteous.

Approaching Morgan, escorted on his cousin's arm, seemed a poor plan.

Fine hairs on the back of her neck rose and that prickling, miserable sensation of someone following her every movement returned.

"Apology accepted, Mr. Cresswell. "Now, if you'll excuse me, I must go."

She *needed* Morgan.

He'd know what to do about the appearance of young Wardie Ferwinckle in Mountain Home.

According to Morgan's timepiece, the shooting contest was set to begin in less than five minutes. He scanned the crowd, one more time, but couldn't find Dad anywhere.

That irresponsible Zylphia had wrought some serious damage to a punctual, responsible, dutiful man.

Morgan shook his head, drew a breath, and, hands on his hips, surveyed the gathering crowd, prepared targets nailed to thick backdrops of hay. On this east edge of town facing east, the likelihood of accidental injury—since everybody knew the shooting contest was always held here on the Fourth—was markedly reduced.

Behind him, the sun inched toward the horizon. Days were long this time of year, and so was the list of entertainments. It would be two hours yet before the light faded appreciably and at least three until the fireworks began.

Something happened—not a gunshot—he would've heard that, even over the din of voices. An argument? A fistfight?

In the street, blocked from his view by at least twenty or thirty men and their families, a commotion arose. Voices surged. A dog barked in rapid warning.

Out of habit, Morgan settled his hand on the grip of his pistol. He searched the crowd, instantly worried about Dad. And Zylphia. But mostly, for Lizzy.

Confusion worsened. The crowd pushed right through the rope barrier, dragging the sawhorses, pulling the devices onto their sides. Children cried. A woman screamed.

Morgan drew, ready to fire, and ran into the melee while most folks—women, children, men carrying little ones, ran past in the opposite direction, desperate to get away.

Until he knew the law had matters in hand, until he'd found Lizzy, Dad, and Zylphia, he had no choice.

Ten

Though half an hour had passed, and the four of them were safely returned to the Hudson home, Liz's hands still shook.

She'd done everything she could to calm Mother, finally given up on that lost cause, but had persuaded Mr. Hudson to open his shirt and expose the bullet wound on his side.

Mr. Hudson had been *shot.*

"We need to call for the doctor." Mother had repeated her demand no fewer than five times.

"No doctor. I don't need a doctor. Save him for those others who need him more." George winced as Liz pressed the cold, wet cloth against his wound.

Absently, she noted Mr. Hudson's blood on the cuff of her new gingham dress. She'd have to soak it out before laundry day.

On her hands, beneath her nails, she saw visions of blood that wasn't there. *Father's blood.* She shivered in December's chill, the slushy mud on the road beneath Father's cooling body seeping through her skirts.

No. *No.*

She wouldn't remember. Not now. She had to stop Mr. Hudson's bleeding. He allowed her to clean the gash on his side and press soft, cotton toweling against the slice that welled blood.

Had the bullet grazed his side, never entering his body? If only they'd be so lucky.

"Tell me again what happened." Morgan halted in his pacing.

"A fellow grabbed Zylphia," Mr. Hudson repeated for the third or fourth time. "I saw a man draw, take aim."

Mr. Hudson no doubt believed that's what he saw. More than likely, though, someone bumped into Mother. Someone aimed, and in the crowd, it looked like Mother was the target.

"In the crowd." Morgan palmed the back of his neck, tugging the tight muscles.

"In the crowd." George repeated. "He *drew.* On *Zylphia.* You can't expect me to stand by."

Not much interest in the annual shooting contest survived after shots were fired in the crowd, so everyone disbanded. Whoever was responsible for shots fired had fled easily in the stampede.

"I can't listen to this gruesome story." Mother fluttered her hands near her face, distress and panic melding into one high-strung worry.

If Elizabeth saw Father's blood, remembered his cooling body beneath her hands as she'd pressed her petticoats against his chest wound to staunch the blood—what must Mother remember?

Mr. Hudson's bleeding slowed—finally. The bullet had carved a furrow in the skin. No puncture wound. *Thank God.*

Morgan's father had told her as much, back on the town green, but there had been *so much blood*. Pandemonium. Terror. Screaming women and crying children. People running in *every* direction.

Elizabeth held the damaged skin together, and working quickly, stitched the edges together.

If Mr. Hudson had stood differently, if the shooter had aimed a little to the left, Mr. Hudson would've been gut-shot. A death sentence.

Dead.

Murdered by gunfire. In the street.

Just like her own father.

In a fit of hysterics, Mother shrieked. "George! *Why* would you do such a thing?" She dropped to her knees in a pillow of skirts. "You know I can't live with another shooting. You *know* I can't..."

Elizabeth ignored her mother, concentrated on the job that had to be done, and pulled another stitch through skin.

"Woman—" George clenched his teeth, obviously in pain. "I hit what I aim for."

"I won't have you engaging in gun-play, Mr. Hudson." Mother's panic rose, frantic.

"What did you think, when I told you I'm a gunsmith? I've been around guns since I was a child. Did you think I'd not know how to handle one of my own make?"

The battle continued for three more stitches,

then four.

Morgan turned from the range, his jaw set. He plunked down the pan of steaming water he'd boiled. In one glance, Elizabeth took in his anger. He held onto his temper by a thread.

Morgan turned to go, but whirled back. To her utter surprise, he picked her up by the waist and set her aside. "I'll do this myself."

He took up the needle and with precision and accuracy—why did he know how to sew?—whipped the stitches into place. Good stitches. Even stitches. "Take your mother upstairs."

Elizabeth washed her shaking hands in the kitchen sink. She lathered with ample soap, washing George Hudson's blood away, but the ghost of Father's blood remained. Deep in the creases of her palms, clotting beneath her fingernails. The shakes intensified and she knew from experience it'd be a good long while until they subsided.

With her back to the room, she clung to the sink, Morgan's rejection stinging.

She stared at her hands. Forced herself to see they were clean.

But clean wasn't good enough, was it?

Mother's voice rose until she shrieked. "I lost my *husband*, George Washington Hudson."

Mother had wailed that same thing at every creditor who came to the door, at both sons, and at Elizabeth.

She'd grown so weary of that excuse—

She squeezed her eyes shut. Tight as they'd go. But nothing could block out the horror in Mother's voice or the memories. *Nothing* buried the memories.

The pungent odor of blood struck Elizabeth with the force of a locomotive at full speed. Salty, tangy, metallic. Her gorge rose and she fought to hold it back. She couldn't move if she wanted to—couldn't run for the back and the necessary—not with memories nailing her feet to the floor.

Mother caught her breath. "The father of my children, my beloved Elijah Speare."

This had to stop. *Mother had to stop.* Elizabeth forced her feet free, turned, and caught Mother by the shoulders. "Stop. This is not Mr. Hudson's fault."

Tears streamed down Elizabeth's face, tears she couldn't control, but she didn't care. Morgan must have finished the stitches. He stood back two steps, his hands red with blood.

But Mother didn't stop. "He bled out," Mother accused. "Into the dirt of a St. Louis street. He *died* because of a bullet."

Mr. Hudson, kind and gentle man that he was, stood, clutching an arm to his injured side. He took Mother's hands, and waited until she met his eye. "I'm sorry, Zee, for all you lost."

"You *don't...understand.*"

"I know a thing or two about burying a spouse. I've lived through that nightmare myself."

"Did she die by a gun?" Mother was in high form now. Her voice raised, her tone shrill.

Elizabeth risked a glance at Morgan. He'd folded his arms, standing behind his father as if guarding his back.

Maybe he was doing just that.

"No, Zee. Cancer. You remember. I wrote you. Told you she lost her life to cancer."

"*My* husband, father of my sons and

daughter..." Mother screamed. "Men drew and fired—and my dearest Elijah was between them. He took a bullet," she sobbed—a sound so ugly and so filled with pain— "and he *died*."

Until this...*this shooting*...Mother had been deliriously happy. Overjoyed. She'd known precisely what Mr. Hudson did for a living and found it acceptable. But Mr. Hudson didn't know Mother. Not really. He didn't know, *couldn't* know, how volatile her moods, how frantic the swings from happy to sad to happy again. He'd seen only the good.

Now that Mother's vitriol made an appearance, everything would change.

The Hudsons wouldn't want either of them.

Liz clamped a hand over her mouth to stifle her own screams.

Like mother, like daughter.

"You don't understand me," Mother accused, wailing with grief and anger and aggravation. "I can't wed a man who won't understand me."

"Zee, darling," Mr. Hudson, so calm, so loving, responded to Mother with patience she didn't deserve. "I didn't say I wouldn't try to understand."

"It doesn't matter." Mother wrenched free. "Come, Elizabeth Louise. Pack our trunks. We are leaving."

Morgan couldn't claim to know Zylphia Speare well, but he *did* know his own dad. He didn't need words to identify the panic and pain in his father's posture and voice at the threat by his crazy, grieving, frantic bride.

The old bat loved her dead husband more than she loved George W. Hudson—but that couldn't be helped. No matter. Dad loved the woman.

"Mrs. Speare," Morgan said, in as soothing a tone as he knew how, "Please, sit. I'll make you a pot of tea."

Mama had loved tea. Found it soothing, calming, just the thing whenever she'd become overwrought. Overwrought to Tildie Hudson had been a spring day compared to Zylphia Speare's typhoon.

Mama and Zylphia couldn't be more different.

Mama had *never* threatened to leave.

But leave, she had. Through no choice of her own. It didn't take a fancy university degree to see Dad's greatest fear was that this woman would leave him too.

"Tea?" Zee shrieked. "I don't want tea."

"What do you want?" he challenged.

Everything Lizzy had told him about her mother's life in the orphanage, her fears of being alone, all came back to him. He didn't want to understand this high-strung woman, didn't want to feel compassion for her, but he tried telling his heart that, and the stubborn organ wouldn't agree.

Compassion flooded, overwhelmed, nearly drowned him. This woman coped, not well, but the best she possibly could in this circumstance. Who was he to expect more?

"I want..." she paced four long strides toward the door, then four long strides back. "I want to live in *peace*. I want a town without gunfights in the street. I want to be safely married without a pistol or rifle taking my husband from me."

Dad's shoulders rounded as he sat in the ladder-back chair at the table. The man was too young to look so old.

"That bullet wasn't meant for me, Zylphia." Dad spoke loudly enough, his pacing, frantic bride should've heard.

But the woman kept muttering, kept stomping back and forth, back and forth.

Dad glanced up, held Morgan's gaze.

In that moment, he saw the import of what Dad said.

What had his old man seen?

"What do you mean?" He headed for his father, ready to resume stitching the wound, if only to better hear what he had to say.

Whatever nervous condition Zylphia had, her daughter seemed to have grown up *without* the family inheritance, so to speak. Thank God for small favors.

Clear as day, he knew that to be true. But now wasn't the time to dwell on that good fortune.

Though tension lined her cheeks, her jaw set with determination, Liz sat her mother in a chair beside Dad.

The older woman collapsed, nearly wilted, and threw herself into her daughter's arms.

If Morgan had to live with drama like that, he'd just as soon remain unmarried the rest of his life.

Thank goodness Dad had seen Zylphia with all her frantic, nervous hysteria before he put his ring on her finger.

Zylphia opened her mouth to continue her tirade but Liz gently placed fingertips over her mother's mouth. "It's time for silence. Mr. Hudson has heard everything you've said. Now he has something of grave importance to tell us."

Zylphia nodded, puckered her lips as if she'd bitten into a lemon, and waited.

Dad turned to Liz for a moment, then to his would-be bride, and took her trembling hand in his. "Zylphia, you must listen."

She blinked at him, her expression vacant. Seconds passed. She finally nodded.

"That bullet was not meant for me." Dad's voice quavered.

Morgan's fists tightened at his sides. He wanted to leap into the conversation, demand information, ensure his dad said it all. They didn't have time to waste on a woman with the vapors.

But Dad waited.

He loves her. Dad, despite the love-of-a-lifetime he'd had with Ma, Dad had fallen in love with this frantic wreck of a woman. Based on today's disaster, he'd obviously give his life for her.

"I saw him aim, Zee," Dad stated plainly. "You were right between him and me. I saw him raise his weapon, take careful aim at your back—"

Liz sucked in a great draw of breath. She clamped a hand over her mouth, as if to stifle a scream.

The flood of compassion he'd felt for Zylphia extended more than far enough to encompass Lizzy Lou. How could he resist? He pulled her to him. Her little frame shook with panic, with the news no one could bear to hear.

She smelled of sunshine and roses. That fragrance he'd forever associate with her.

"Who, Dad?" Who would shoot a woman—

this woman—in the middle of Mountain Home, with hundreds of people around?

"I don't know him." Emotion choked Dad, the most pain he'd heard in the old man's voice since Ma died. He must've been frantic, watching a gunman shoot his beloved...

Had that been his Lizzy, why—

Morgan clutched her tighter, pressed a kiss to her hair, praying and cursing, grieving and relieved.

The cacophony of emotions stirred up sediment he didn't want to revisit. Old muck at the bottom of a personal riverbed that needed to stay put. Nothing—*nothing*—troubled him as much as the inability to act, to fix things. To correct the course life had taken.

"I don't understand." Liz's voice, muffled against his chest, prompted him to release her, but not all the way.

"You must be mistaken, Mr. Hudson." She shook her head, vehement denial—the most frantic he'd seen Lizzy, ever. Compared to her mother, she was as calm as a summer's day. Composed. Contained. "*Why* would anyone shoot my mother?"

"That's what I want to know." Morgan held Liz at arm's length. A glimmer of something flashed through her eyes. "What aren't you telling me?"

Secrets. Damning secrets.

Shadows had flickered through Arrah's gaze in those last weeks before she'd left him, sending her engagement ring and a vague note to the house. She'd pulverized his heart, shattered it against the cold, hard reality of secrets she'd kept.

Did he have the right to demand answers of

Lizzy? She wasn't his bride, hadn't agreed to wed him. They'd only begun.

But if they were to have a future, he had to ask.

"Mrs. Speare," he turned to her neurotic mother. "Why would someone want to shoot you?"

The old woman's eyes rounded. She clung to Dad's hand with the kind of fear that couldn't be feigned. "I don't know!"

"We four will figure this out." He'd had enough skirting the issue. Enough secrets. *Enough.*

Dusk was beginning to fall. Before long, the fireworks show would begin—if anyone dared attend after that supposedly random shooting—and the firecrackers popping could cover a whole lot of shooting going on elsewhere in town.

Morgan shut the curtains in the kitchen. He'd not have anyone looking through the windows into the lit room and watching them.

Liz was quick to see the need, and within thirty seconds, the windows were covered, the panes shut against listening ears, and four chairs pulled up, around the kitchen table.

Morgan was the last to take his seat. He held Dad's eye, nodded in solidarity. Dad wanted this solved too. He wanted to know who'd shot at his bride as badly as Morgan did.

"No one leaves until we put our heads together and figure out who and why someone intended to harm you, Mrs. Speare." He fought for calm. He ignored Elizabeth's little hand as it settled on his forearm. He flexed, reacting too strongly to her touch on his bare skin.

"Who wanted you dead badly enough to come to Mountain Home and risk shooting in front of a potential hundred witnesses?"

Mrs. Speare's mouth worked, but nothing came out. She turned to her daughter. "I—I don't know."

"Mother, it's time to admit Papa may have been shot by his business partner." She turned to Morgan, all reticence and secrets banished. "I saw him in town. Earlier today."

"Who?" Dad asked. "Your father's business partner?"

"Wardie Ferwinckle. I can think of no reason for him to be here, none at all, unless he shot and killed my father, and now he's here after us."

Eleven

The moment the statement left her lips, she knew she'd made a mistake. "You must recall Papa's partner, Wardie Ferwinckle, is *not* the only one that could want to see us come to harm."

Morgan shrugged, as if to say, *I don't see who.*

"What about your former housekeeper? Miss Dimond?"

He waved that away, almost as fast as his father did.

"Have you forgotten the day I interrupted her at the shop? She was beside herself—"

Apparently, Morgan hadn't taken the unstable woman seriously—but Elizabeth had. She'd seen enough from her own mother to know how frantic and unhinged a woman could become when her heart was broken.

"I had every reason to dismiss her!" Mother pushed out of Elizabeth's arms and sat upright. "Elizabeth Louise, you saw the way she looked at my George Hudson, didn't you? I couldn't have that woman in my house, couldn't have her continue to work for us. Why, she'd slit my throat in my sleep."

"Ina Dimond wouldn't hurt a fly." Morgan dismissed Mother, and her fears, out of hand.

Why had Elizabeth ever entertained a future with the man? He hadn't a brain between his ears. "You know full well your beloved Miss Dimond loves your father."

"She does?" Mr. Hudson perked up. A confused smile ghosted across his lips.

"Yes," Elizabeth insisted, but she wasn't happy. "She does. She's livid that you invited Mother here, that you've been writing to her all this time."

Morgan shook his head, dismissing it all— *again*.

"You're foolish to ignore the obvious," she told him.

"You don't know Ina like I do."

How had she ever thought this man different?

"We're getting nowhere." Morgan pushed back his chair and stood. "Dad, I'm going for the sheriff. We need help to bring in Mr. Ferwinckle."

"And Miss Dimond." Elizabeth insisted.

Morgan shot her a hot glare, full of impatience. "Who held the gun, Dad? Man, or woman?"

"Man."

Morgan gestured grandly as if to say, *See*?

"Anybody would be a fool to implicate

themselves in front of an entire town. But anyone could have hired that gunman, whomever he was, and now he's long gone. Probably lit out as soon as the commotion was over."

"Maybe."

Morgan might've been quick, just now, to admit she'd had a good idea, but she wasn't ready to forgive. Or forfeit the win. "If you're going to have the sheriff bring in Mr. Ferwinckle you'll need my help. You haven't the vaguest idea what he looks like."

"I don't want you on the street. You're in danger."

"So are you!"

"I'm a man!"

Elizabeth returned his grand, *See?*, and tapped her foot. She counted past ten and all the way to twenty before she stood. Sometimes she really hated looking all the way up, up, up to his much greater height. "I'll have you recall," she spat, too angry to keep his stupid cousin's threats a secret one moment longer. "Miss Dimond and Mr. Ferwinckle are far from the only possibilities of who'd like to see Mother and me gone."

"Is that so?"

She glared at Morgan. "How quickly you forget your favorite cousin and his misbehavior in the shop a few days ago. I refused to allow him to escort me to the events today. Remember? He approached me on the street shortly before the shooting. I had an awful feeling someone was watching me while Ray spoke to me. Was he identifying me for a shooter?"

The smug expression disappeared from Morgan's features. "Ray?"

"Yes, Ray. Who else? How many favorite cousins do you have?"

He waved that away. All pretense of anger forgotten. "Why didn't you tell me?"

"When?"

His frustration and superiority disappeared. He looked at her with compassion and gentleness...and like he'd scoop her into his arms and hold on tight.

Ah, now she remembered why she'd considered a tomorrow—maybe a lifetime—with this man.

"What did he say?"

"He apologized. Sincere enough, I suppose. But something, *somebody*, was watching me while Ray was *right there*."

Morgan thrust both hands into his hair, grabbed great hanks of it and tugged. When he left off, his hair stood up at wild angles—so different than that morning when, crisply groomed, he'd offered her his arm to walk out together toward the day's celebratory events.

"You're coming with me." He seized Elizabeth's upper arm and marched her to the door.

If she hadn't wanted to go along, she'd have put up a fight.

But she did want to go.

"Dad, lock up. Arm yourselves. We'll be back as fast as possible."

Twelve

With Lizzy close beside him, Morgan strode at a fast pace to the sheriff's office. No telling if he'd be there, but they had to start somewhere.

One thing they hadn't considered—Dad might think somebody aimed at Zee, but Morgan thought it more likely somebody took aim at Dad, and Zylphia, flighty thing that she was, stepped into the line of fire, then out again, just in time for Dad to take a bullet. Thank God, the bullet barely grazed his skin.

One thing still chafed. What was Ray playing at? Morgan had known that man all his life. Loved him, but knew his shortcomings—and that man apologized to no one. He didn't believe, not for one second, that Ray would apologize for bad behavior...unless it was a front for something else.

Especially as it happened during the one time

Morgan wasn't at Lizzy's side, all day long. Whole thing gave Morgan a real bad feeling.

"You're sure. About Ray and that prickly sense..." Just like when he'd lost his mother, helpless to fight a monster he couldn't see or lock his fists around, Lizzy could've been snatched from him.

Before he'd ever had the chance—

"I've had it up to here—" She swept one blade of a hand across her forehead, the high-water mark, he supposed. "You, *Mr. Hudson*, are un*believable.*"

Worked up, but nothing like the shrew her mother turned into when riled. Elizabeth—*his Lizzy*—was hurt. He'd somehow cut her to the quick. He'd never meant to. "That's not what I meant—"

"Stop." She brushed past him, her boots striking the boardwalk planks with crisp, even reports.

In the distance, the first fireworks erupted against an indigo sky.

To less-honed ears, either one sounded a bit too much like gunfire.

"Wait." He slipped his hand about her upper arm, pulled her around. She came easily into his arms, and he simply held her, savored her warmth and the movement of breath in and out of her lungs.

Vibrant and animated with life.

He drew a deep breath of her rose-scented hair. He smoothed his hands over those blue gingham sleeves, savoring her warmth beneath. "I can't lose you. Could've been you today, in that crowd."

His throat closed. He squeezed his eyes shut, tried to block his overactive imagination. Her pretty blue gingham dress spattered with red blood, her face as pale as Ma's had been at the end.

"You believe me?" She spoke so quietly, he barely heard.

He clung to her all the tighter. "Of course, I believe you."

"But—" She pushed against his chest.

He didn't want to let her go, but he did. Her eyes met his, open wide, searching, every emotion plain as day in their blue depths. But light was fading fast, and in moments he wouldn't be able to make out the subtle shifts of emotion.

"Why wouldn't I believe you? You said Ray apologized, but something was off. So, something's off." Anger at his stupid cousin flushed hot and fast and overwhelming. "I find out he put your life in danger, and I'll kill him with my bare hands."

Lizzy flinched. "Why? He's your cousin. You l-love him."

He ought to keep a look out. It wouldn't do to be so wrapped up in this lady that any one of their supposed enemies could come out of a shadowed alleyway between buildings and finish the job they'd started. Dad and Zee were counting on them to bring the law in on their troubles.

But nothing was half as important as Lizzy.

In that moment, he couldn't remember his manners. He hadn't the patience to woo her gently.

He kissed her.

Hard. Quick. Desperate to convince his soul the woman he loved yet lived.

She must've been in shock. She stood, stiff in his arms while he kissed her like a brute.

A second passed and his conscience nearly convinced him he'd gone about this all wrong.

But then, all of a sudden, she kissed him back. Her arm looped around his neck as she pulled his head down and leveraged herself up higher to meet him. He nearly laughed aloud as she used his boots for a step-stool.

His heart sang with arresting joy and he lost himself in the eagerness of her kiss.

"Lizzy—"

Her kiss claimed his mouth again, in two short bursts. "I'm mad at you."

He'd been downright mad at her—about something. Serious, too.

Fireworks in the distance erupted in close succession. Muted whistles and applause filtered on the cooling breeze.

A gunshot whistled through the air. Nearby.

Unmistakable—Colt six-shooter.

Ten feet away. Twenty, at most. *Close! Much* too close.

Terror sank poisonous fangs deep.

He shoved Lizzy down, threw himself in front of her, a shield.

Morgan's hand closed over the butt of his pistol.

Another shot—in warning? Fired into the air?

The Peacemaker cleared leather, and he zeroed in on target.

"Drop your weapon." Sheriff Liam Talmadge. Morgan's pistol aimed straight at the sheriff's heart.

Sheriff. Smoking six-gun in his grip.

Morgan's heart pounded, way too fast. If the law had turned bad, they were *all* dead.

"Drop it, Morgan." The sheriff's aim was true. Better than most.

No respectable gunsmith threw his weapon in the dust. He stuffed the pistol in its holster and raised his hands.

Lizzy squirmed beneath him on the boardwalk. "Get *off* me."

He ignored her. No sense dropping the only shield she had until he knew which way the wind blew. "Sheriff Talmadge." Morgan squinted in the slowly darkening street. "That you shooting at us?"

"*At* you?"

Might as well find out. "Yessir."

"Boy, if I'd shot at you, you'd be bleeding all over Mrs. Whipple's Bakery boardwalk."

"You're holding the smoking gun."

"Don't sass me, Morgan Hudson. I fired a warning shot at the moon, in fair warning."

"Warning?" Another quick look up and down the street—nothing. Everybody who was out was at the fireworks, six blocks down, near the town green.

"Law's on the books, son. You're in clear violation, kissing like that on Mountain Home's city streets."

Lizzy shoved harder, and satisfied she wasn't in imminent danger, he pushed to his feet and pulled her up against him.

"We were headed to the jail, Sheriff." Lizzy cut to the reason for their outing. "To report a crime. We need your help."

"Later, Miss Speare. You two are under arrest." Liam Talmadge wasn't one to joke. The old man hadn't pulled a prank...*ever*.

"Since when," Morgan asked, "is kissing

illegal?"

"Since the day this fair city was incorporated. The law clearly states kissing—like that—on city streets is punishable by two days in jail."

"Two days!" Lizzy whirled from Sheriff to Morgan. "That's ridiculous. Why, it's—"

"Unless, of course, the kissin' is done by married folk. Who could blame you, then?"

"—preposterous!" Lizzy sputtered. "I've never heard of such a thing."

"I'm gonna have to take you two in. Might as well start your sentence tonight."

"I can't. We can't. Sheriff—a gunman fired on my mother this afternoon in the crowd, when the melee interrupted the shooting contest."

"She hurt?"

"Well, no—"

"Come along quiet like, Miss Speare."

"—but Mr. Hudson was shot in the belly."

The Sheriff looked Morgan over, apparently searching for indication he'd been gut-shot. Morgan would've laughed if he weren't irritated. "My father, Sheriff. Grazed just under the rib. Cartridge dug out a trough nearly a quarter-inch deep."

"He won't be attending the wedding." The sheriff shook his head. "That's a shame."

"What wedding?" Lizzy's remarkable blue eyes narrowed.

"Hudson." Sheriff Talmadge's attention never left Lizzy's face. "I can understand the draw, you choosing this lively, pretty gal for your bride, but she really ain't the brightest star in the sky, now is she?"

Lizzy gasped in outrage. "No matter what

your law says in this town, Sheriff, we are *not* engaged to be married."

Not what a man wanted to hear—though he'd far rather have her for a wife than a stepsister—and she had a distinct possibility of turning out just like her Ma, *and* he'd barely kissed her once.

Must she act like a shotgun marriage—to him—would be a terrible thing? Hadn't *she* kissed *him* as if she couldn't bear to lose him?

Lizzy raised her chin. "I'll take my sentence and sit in your jail for two days."

"Fine then. Git a move on." Sheriff Talmadge resettled his hat more firmly in place. "When your two days are up—and two nights, too, I'll hear your complaints about whatever that hoopla was about on main street."

"You can't mean to wait two days to hear testimony about the shooters—" Since when had Talmadge been such a stickler?

"Indeed I do." He spat a stream of tobacco juice into weeds peeking from beneath the boardwalk. "Absolutely do."

Absurd. "Why?"

"Them's the laws, Hudson. Improper kissing on city streets of Mountain Home earns the guilty parties forty-eight hours locked up—apart from one another, mind you—and no hearing of complaints for the full forty-eight hours."

"You made that part up!" Lizzy had the roar of a lion.

If circumstances weren't so dire, Morgan would have scooped her up and kissed her again. "My Dad's life is at stake, Sheriff."

"My mother," Lizzy quickly added. "M-my mother's in danger. I saw my father's business partner in town, earlier today—he's here, I just know it—"

"Sounds like," Talmadge cut her off, even as he widened his stance and rocked back onto his heels, "you two'd better be glad the law makes an exception for married folk. We'll find the J.P., get you two hitched, then see what all this is about."

Lizzy turned to Morgan, skeptical and furious.

He didn't like that look in her eye.

"Sheriff Talmadge, you'll make an exception. This once."

He understood how she felt. No one told him what to do. Not if they wanted him to actually do it.

It seemed Lizzy was of a like mind.

If *he* said no...refused marriage, then maybe she'd be all for it. She might be mad as a wet hen, for awhile, but then she'd be his. Once they ironed out the trouble.

"No." He told Talmadge. "Lock me up. Do what you've got to do—right after you apprehend the trigger-happy fools running around Mountain Home. But nobody's getting married today."

The sheriff clanged the cell door shut, tested the lock, and without looking back, left the jail. At least he'd assured Elizabeth he'd be back, as quickly as possible—not with the J.P., but with their list of suspects.

Crazy old coot.

She didn't believe, not for one minute, that Mountain Home had a law on the books about public kissing. So why he'd left her with Morgan, in the same cell, where any crazy gun-toting fool could shoot them dead, she didn't know.

People passed by outside in the dark, making a nuisance of themselves. The fireworks must have ended.

She gripped the iron bars and leaned her forehead against one. She forced herself to calm down.

She would *not* behave like Mother, who would have stood up to Morgan, right then and there. *You can't kiss me like that, Morgan Hudson, then say you don't want me.*

She should've said yes and demanded the sheriff fetch the J.P.

But that would've made her as pathetic as Mother, begging the man she loved to love her in return.

She'd done the right thing.

Hadn't she?

Thirteen

"Everybody, settle down." Sheriff Talmadge bellowed at the significant gathering inside the tiny jail.

Morgan, in the first of two cells with both Lizzy and Miss Ina Dimond, scanned each face. One of those present *must* be the guilty party.

Trying not to be too obvious, Morgan kept a close eye on Elijah Speare's partner, Wardie Ferwinckle. And his own cousin, Ray. The two men both seemed properly shamed. Ray sat on the bare tick, his hands between his knees, his head bowed.

The dentist, Ferwinckle, leaned against the far wall. Hard to believe a boy that young could be a professional, bonafide dentist, but Mrs. Speare, who'd just arrived with Dad—and waited on the freedom side of the bars with Sheriff Talmadge for the outcome of the questioning, verified that the young man was, indeed, her late husband's partner and a real dentist.

"Now," the sheriff said, "I want to know, right now, Wardie Ferwinckle, why you're in my town. You tell the whole truth, boy, or I swear you won't like the consequences."

Wardie removed his pocket book from inside his coat, opened it, and pulled out a stack of greenbacks an inch thick.

Whistles of appreciation echoed through the brick building. Morgan had seen a lot of stupid things in his life, but this had to be the dumbest.

Did the boy want to find himself robbed on the way out of town?

"I came to Mountain Home," Wardie insisted, "to give Widow Speare this money—money I managed to salvage from the failing business."

"Where'd it come from?" Talmadge opened his hand and Wardie, trusting as the day was long—*idiot fool*—passed the stack of bills through the bars.

Talmadge held one up to the light. If a forgery, Talmadge didn't say anything.

"I know Elijah would've wanted his sons to have a chance at university. He'd want his family cared for. I don't need the money, so I thought…"

"What?" Talmadge handed the money to Mrs. Speare. "You thought the money would assuage your guilty conscience?"

"I did nothing wrong!"

"Didn't you, now."

"No. I didn't kill Elijah Speare, and I didn't steal a dime from him. But the money was gone, just the same."

"Uh-*huh*. What money?"

The sheriff did a fine job questioning the witnesses, or the defendants, whatever they were, so Morgan watched everybody else closely. Someone would give themselves away.

"My grandpa paid Dr. Speare a fair buy-in. To take me on as an apprentice, so I'd own a share of the business. It's not illegal, Sheriff. It's what's done. See, an established dentist has patients, equipment, an operating business. He doesn't just give that to a new graduate."

Mrs. Speare humphed. "Why didn't you offer us this money months ago, when we needed it?"

Wardie gripped the bars. "I've only salvaged it recently. It takes time to collect outstanding debts. When I saw the balance in the bank account, I decided to bring as much money to you as possible."

"You could've kept it for yourself." Mrs. Speare opened Dad's jacket and tucked it all inside, in plain view of everybody in the jailhouse and half the people gathering on the sidewalk.

Morgan nearly rolled his eyes. Did Zylphia want to see Dad pummeled on the way home? Attacked for the absurd amount of cash in his coat pocket?

"Or," Wardie argued, "I could ensure my partner's widow and children are cared for. It's only decent."

"His children are older than you." Talmadge, apparently, played devil's advocate.

"I have everything I need. If you met my parents, my grandparents...you'd see more money won't change a thing."

Morgan mentally crossed young Wardie off the list of suspects. No way was the fellow guilty of anything.

"Make way. Move aside." A booming male voice cleared the congestion of onlookers from the jailhouse door. Mr. Harold Bayliss, filthy rich miner—and the man who'd stolen Arrah's fickle heart, strode inside...his fickle-hearted wife trailing behind.

What were the Baylisses doing here? Morgan hadn't mentioned them to Talmadge as suspects.

Harold Bayliss was dressed in all the finery of his station...as was Arrah. Morgan would've waged a constant battle, every day, keeping that woman's dressmaker paid.

The glittering diamonds on Mrs. Bayliss's ring finger were ostentatious and made the expensive, tasteful engagement ring he'd presented look like a pauper's gift.

Morgan hadn't seen it at the time, but he'd dodged a bullet.

He forced himself to nod in greeting, first at Bayliss, then at Arrah. Her lips pursed as if seeing him behind bars made her inappropriately happy.

"You require our assistance, Sheriff?" Bayliss offered the lawman his hand. "We returned to the house, and discovered your message."

The house. All thirty rooms. Morgan tried not to scowl.

Bayliss, the pompous glutton, glared at Morgan even as he released the sheriff's handshake.

"Indeed, I do, Harold. See, I'm looking under every stone, behind every bush."

Harold clasped his coat, nodded his head...as if he'd been born with a silver spoon in his mouth instead of having made his millions dragging silver out of the mountains between grubby hands.

"I have it on good authority," Talmadge shifted to better address Bayliss, "you saw Mr. Hudson in the hour before the shooting contest and issued a challenge."

Harold Bayliss barked a laugh. "Who told you that?"

Talmadge, more skilled at interrogation than Morgan had thought, smiled—a friendly, man-to-man smile that put Bayliss at ease.

Lizzy turned to Morgan to whisper, "Who is that?"

"Bayliss. Big mine."

She shrugged.

The short answer would do. He indicated Arrah with his chin.

Arrah, still a willowy blonde, did resemble Lizzy, but was so much *less*. Less pretty, less bright, less spirited. Just...*less*.

And to think he'd believed, not so long ago, he wanted Arrah for his wife.

He leaned close so no one would overhear. "She left me for Bayliss."

Lizzy's eyes rounded. She mouthed, *wife*?

He shook his head, watched relief steal across Lizzy's beautiful face, and took a king-sized risk. He linked his pinkie finger with hers, half-expecting her to pull away.

"Long time ago," he whispered.

Sheriff Talmadge chuckled. "Glad to hear it. You know how talk is."

Harold smiled the smug grin of a man everybody wanted to be.

Ha.

"So you won't mind telling me exactly what

your problem is with the Hudsons. And the Speares."

Harold glanced from Dad, to Morgan, to the sheriff. "Who are the Speares?"

Both Lizzy and her mother raised their hands as if children in a schoolroom.

Bayliss dismissed them with the slightest of glances. "I don't know the Speares, so they are of no consequence. The Hudsons," Bayliss said, ripe with disdain, "are fools. No law against disliking fools, is there, Sheriff?"

Morgan's hackles rose, but he remained silent. Dad shifted, but didn't speak.

Even Mrs. Speare had the good sense to hold her tongue.

The sheriff chuckled. "Can't say there is."

Anybody who didn't know the lawman would think he rather liked the wealthy man. But a gunsmith couldn't help but have lots to do with lawmen. If the Hudsons weren't supplying weapons, identifying pieces, providing expert testimony, or working together to solve a crime, the sheriff dropped by to purchase cartridges or warn them about somebody coming through town.

Bayliss wouldn't know that. Morgan doubted Bayliss knew much of anything.

"If Mrs. Bayliss and I are not needed further," Bayliss said, in a cat-got-the-cream manner anybody normal would detest, "we'll say goodnight."

The crowd at the door parted but Morgan didn't bother to watch them exit.

Something wasn't quite right with Arrah and the way she stood a distance from her husband, or the furtive glances she cast him...but that wasn't

Morgan's problem. Unless they were behind the day's trouble.

Talmadge didn't seem to think so. The lawman drew a deep breath, turned back to the rest of the crowd gathered. He took in Ray Cresswell, still sitting on the cot. Interesting that Ray hadn't acknowledged his first cousin—on the other side—and she hadn't acknowledged him.

Morgan used the excuse to tug Lizzy near by her pinkie finger. "Ray Cresswell is first cousins with Bayliss's wife, Arrah Cresswell Bayliss. Other side of the family."

"You were engaged to your cousin's cousin?"

He shrugged. At least Lizzy's anger at him had been set aside. For now.

And she still let him hold onto her. By the pinkie.

"I've spoken at length with Miss Dimond," Talmadge announced, "four times this week, so let's just say I know all about the bad blood between the Hudson family and her."

Ina sniffed.

Morgan rested a soothing hand on her shoulder.

"Ina?" The sheriff approached the cell, met her eye and showed her surprising kindness. "Did you cause trouble for the Hudsons?"

"No! Of course not. I might've told a few people what they did, how that high-and-mighty Mrs. Speare fired me for no good reason, but I wouldn't hurt the Hudsons."

"Did you do something to hurt Mrs. Speare?"

"No!"

"Her daughter?"

"No."

"I believe you." Talmadge reached through the bars to squeeze Ina's hand.

After a moment, he pulled away—and the supposedly locked cell squeaked open.

Somebody chuckled.

Ray glanced up, finally.

If *anybody* in this circus looked guilty... "Ray?" Morgan released Lizzy and approached the bars separating them. "Want to tell me what's going on here?"

Ray shook his head, his attention firmly back on his knotted hands.

"You and I have been friends since we sat on our mamas' laps in long dresses. I treated you too well the day you came into the shop and bothered my lady. So *talk*."

Everyone waited in silence.

Seconds passed. Ray finally looked up. "I swear, Morgan, I didn't do anything. I felt terrible about treating Miss Speare with disrespect. So, I apologized. That's all."

Morgan stared at his cousin, saw nothing but truth in the other man's eyes.

"And you waited 'til I wasn't at her side, because...?"

"Because I finally saw her in the crowd. You saw the crush of people."

Everybody, even Mrs. Speare, kept quiet.

Either he'd missed something...or everybody inside the jailhouse walls was innocent.

That meant—

"Morgan?" Dad asked, quick on the uptake as ever. He cleared his throat, looked to Zylphia as though she were everything to him.

Talmadge tugged his ear, their predetermined

cue. "I don't like this." Spoken low, so nobody outside overheard.

As though nothing had changed, Morgan sauntered to the cot and sat, all the better to slip his Colt, fully loaded, from beneath the tick between his knees.

Panic pounced on Morgan's back as he gripped the Colt.

A well-lit jail, windows open wide on a hot July night. *Fish in a barrel.*

The hair on the back of his neck stood on end. His pulse pounded.

Talmadge killed the light.

Again, Morgan pushed Lizzy behind him. Smart girl—she moved quietly, easily.

At his back, she clutched his shirt and pressed her face between his shoulder blades. Morgan's heart nearly shattered. He *must* protect the innocent, the weak, the woman he loved.

"What's happening?" Zylphia demanded. "Geo?"

Clueless woman! Her voice came from further down the wall—where Dad had moved them, out of the line of fire. Others shuffled. Clothing brushed the brick floor.

Fish in a—

One rifle shot. The slug whispered between iron bars and struck the brick-and-plaster wall.

—barrel.

Fourteen

Sheriff Talmadge sat on the edge of a chair in his parlor. He scanned the four faces—Mr. Hudson, Mother, Morgan, and herself. Elizabeth held his gaze, though the intensity of this lawman would make anyone flinch.

"You've had half an hour." The lawman was deadly serious. "I want to know exactly what trouble you Hudsons have brought to this town. Speak freely. Get it all out in the open."

By Hudsons, he included Speares. Elizabeth looked to her mother, her fear mounting.

At first, no ideas came. Not for any of them.

"See anybody else you recognize among the visitors?"

Mother shook her head. Elizabeth tried to recall, but everyone here was a stranger. She'd paid so little attention.

Mr. Hudson's side hurt. He favored it as he sat on the sofa. "We have hundreds of migrant miners and migrant field laborers in the valley. I saw hundreds of unfamiliar faces. Could have been any one of them."

"Good. Keep thinking." The sheriff rubbed a thumb over his jaw.

"Murphy's had a theft this week. He mentioned it—" Morgan shook his head, discarding the thought.

Talmadge split a glance between Mr. Hudson and Morgan. "Turn anybody away? Refuse to sell them a pistol? Ammunition?"

"Only Ina."

"Hmm. Any paying customer dissatisfied?"

Morgan snorted, as if such a thing never happened.

The sheriff made a rolling motion with his hand. "Keep the discussion going. Nothing is too unreasonable."

Seconds slipped past. "Miss Speare," the sheriff turned to Elizabeth. "You came to Colorado with your mother. Did you spurn a swain in St. Louis? A man who'd follow you here, angry that you left?"

An easy question to answer. "No."

"Take your time. Think about it."

"I don't need to, sir. There was no one."

Talmadge blinked. "No one?" He checked with her mother, then Morgan.

Just how specifically need she answer the same question? "I've never had a suitor."

Mother shifted on the sofa. Impatient or uncomfortable, or perhaps both. "She had no suitors, gentlemen. None."

Three men turned to Elizabeth, expecting verification.

"Miss Speare, we know how young people are." Talmadge opened his palms, gesturing as if secrets from her mother were nothing to be ashamed of. "Not all courtships occur under a mother's watchful eye."

"I would know!" Mother interrupted, her tone adamant. "Several would-be beaus came to the door, sniffing around Elizabeth's skirts like dogs."

Elizabeth's heart leapt into her throat. To hear Mother speak this way—

"I sent every last one of them away." Mother grew more animated, more agitated. "I sent them away because none were suitable."

Too fast to recognize it, embarrassment changed to horror...with recognition of all Mother admitted with her flippant statement.

She couldn't breathe—her chest locked up and wouldn't work...

Morgan must've comprehended Mother's confession for he reached for her hand and simply held it.

As if she were listening to someone else's story, someone else's unbelievable tale, Mother continued. "Elizabeth is a good girl. She understands her duty."

Mother spoke with pride, with utter certainty in Elizabeth's obedience.

The sheriff must've seen worse perfidy in his work, because he showed no emotion. "Her duty?"

"Elizabeth Louise's responsibility is to me, her mother. She, as my only daughter, is honor-bound to remain at home. To care for me in my old age."

Mother had sent away anyone who'd ever come to their home, anyone who'd ever called on her.

She'd had gentleman callers?

When? Who?

Had anyone, *ever*, been as selfish as her mother?

Elizabeth's ears rang. Her head spun and she feared she'd swoon.

Mother fell quiet, the lawman's question answered.

How could her *mother*—the woman who was supposed to love her—have done this?

Elizabeth focused on breathing. In. Out. In. Out.

Morgan and his father communicated, without words. Minor expressions. Easy for them— they knew one another so well.

"Mrs. Speare," Morgan said, his voice surprisingly gentle. "You can be of help to us. Your keen memory will serve us well."

"I'll certainly try." Mother smiled, her vanity responding so well to Morgan's change in subject.

"Did anyone in St. Louis refuse to obey your edict regarding your daughter? Did they refuse to stay away?"

"No, of course not. They knew their place." She smiled at Morgan's father, pleasure mingling with her relaxed expression. She honestly saw nothing wrong with her behavior—with robbing Elizabeth of freedom, her life, the chance to make a choice for herself.

All this time, for years and years, she'd thought herself uninteresting, unattractive—

"Was anyone in St. Louis jealous of you?" the

sheriff added. "Or your daughter?"

Elizabeth closed her eyes, fighting tears, fighting to remain calm. She'd think about all of this, all it meant, once the fright was over.

"Oh, yes. Plenty of other women were jealous of us. We had a lovely home, the finest of furnishings."

Mother seemed to have forgotten her determination to present herself to Mr. Hudson as a domestic woman, one who loved the simple, and wished to do the housekeeping herself.

"Newest gowns, the most fashionable of invitations—"

Visions of gray dresses, her wardrobe filled with gray in every fabric and every shade—

Elizabeth hadn't wanted dresses. Nor invitations.

She'd wanted to fit in...she'd wanted to be loved. But she'd worn dresses that kept people at a distance, made herself invisible.

Talmadge nodded. "Did your husband, Mrs. Speare, have enemies?"

"Enemies?" The wistful tone disappeared. Mother sat straighter. "Why would Dr. Speare have had enemies?"

The lawman shrugged. "We're turning over every rock, ma'am. I don't know where to look until you help me find it."

"He was loved by all. A wonderful dentist."

Talmadge nodded. "I'm sure he was. Would anyone have wanted to see him hurt? Maybe lose his ability to practice dentistry?"

Mother gaped. "No, of course not. He was shot in the street, but that was an accident. A horrible, terrible accident."

Silence gaped for the space of three or four seconds.

Talmadge leaned forward a little more. "Are you *sure* about that?"

Mother shrieked. In fury, in pain, in the stunned reaction of a widow who just learned her beloved husband would not be coming home.

After all Mr. Hudson had seen, Elizabeth found it no surprise that he showed Mother patience, kindness, and the compassion she so desperately needed. He held her to his shoulder, though he couldn't hide the wince when his stitches pulled.

Nor was Elizabeth surprised when Morgan, the man she'd come to love, followed his father's example. The two men were so much alike. In every way that Mr. Hudson showed love, affection, patience, and commitment for Mother, his son showed those very same traits...for her.

Morgan called her Lizzy Lou. A nickname. A nickname that embodied the love she'd been waiting for, her entire life.

She was in love. Hopelessly and forever, with Morgan Hudson.

In that moment of stark realization, she knew, without a doubt, that she would be alone—and deserve to be alone—not because of Mother's selfishness, but because she had prevented herself from embracing this one chance at everlasting love, this *only* chance that mattered.

Before Morgan, no one ever captured her attention, no one made her yearn for love and affection. Only Morgan.

But she had built a wall, so thick and so high, even his exquisite patience couldn't find a way around it. She'd built that wall with stones—one with every friend's marriage, with every reminder issued by Mother that she was duty-bound to remain at home, with every passing year and every birthday. That wall protected her heart, allowed her to pretend she didn't care that she grew older without hope for love of her own.

She grasped Morgan's hand more tightly and took in his profile.

This man, this one man, was worth the leap into the unknown.

For him, she would choose love over fear.

For him, she would dismantle the walls that kept him out. She'd trust and hope and dream.

"Elizabeth?"

She blinked, and turned to the sheriff, Mr. Talmadge. He'd called her name.

"I'm sorry. What did you say?"

He smiled with kindness, though no doubt aggravated with her wandering mind.

Morgan stroked her hand with his thumb, though he could have no way of knowing the power of the epiphany, the realizations that had forever changed the course of her future.

Mr. Hudson nodded, as if accepting whatever the sheriff had just said. "It's a crazy speculation, but nothing else makes sense."

Morgan must've seen her confusion, and in his kindness, leaned near to repeat. "Whoever shot and killed your father must have followed Wardie Ferwinckle to Mountain Home."

"Oh." A shocking, terrible theory.

"Makes sense, if, whoever that man is, couldn't learn where you and your mother had gone."

"And, theoretically," Morgan's Dad added, "something changed. He might believe you left St. Louis because you feared for your lives."

Oh, no. She and her mother might have, absurd though it seemed, brought calamity to Mountain Home.

"If we're right," the sheriff continued, "and Elijah Speare's death wasn't an accident...and the man who shot him took aim at you today, Mrs. Speare, that means..."

"I'm in danger. Oh, heaven help me. I'm in danger!"

Mother really could be the most selfish person.

"You're safe with us, dearest." Mr. Hudson held her close, ignoring the pain of his wound, concerned only for her safety and her contentment.

How, why, had Mother, despite herself, found a man who loved her so completely?

She must, with her new understanding, apply the same question to herself. How, why, had she, a plain, simple woman who'd shut everyone out for years and years, by the grace of God, found a man who loved her so completely?

She watched Morgan's dear face, drinking in the blink of his eyes, the stubble on his chin, the softness in his expression when he turned to her.

"Zylphia," Mr. Hudson whispered, "no harm will come to you. You know that, don't you?"

"I know nothing of the sort! I was nearly shot *in the back* today. A man aimed a pistol and shot at me!"

"She's not the only one the assassin could be here to eliminate." Morgan's second hand closed around Elizabeth's. Soothing. Strength. An anchor in the storm.

The sheriff glanced at George Hudson, then at her, then to Morgan.

Morgan cleared his throat. "Mr. Ferwinckle. Where is he?"

Oh, no. Papa. Mother, and she. Now Mr. Ferwinckle. For reasons she couldn't comprehend, they were all in danger.

The sheriff grew still. "He went back to the hotel."

Morgan stood, bent to kiss Elizabeth quick and sure. Just as quickly, his attention turned to the sheriff. "We'd best get to him. Fast."

Elizabeth stood—she'd go with. She'd help. She couldn't remain here—

Sheriff Talmadge whipped open the front door of his home and whistled, shrill and brief. A signal, apparently, because a man with a tin star pinned to his vest bolted up the porch steps and inside.

Quicker than two shakes, Sheriff Talmadge informed the deputy to guard his family and the two women.

Despite the fact that Morgan didn't look back as he joined the sheriff and his father, on foot, heading to the hotel—wherever that was—she loved him more than ever.

If Morgan Hudson could run to a stranger's aid, to notify him of danger, she could most certainly unlock the door of the fortified castle in which her heart lived, and let him in.

Fifteen

Morgan followed Dad and the sheriff through the hotel's double doors, his Colt drawn.

The night manager met them at the foot of the stairs. "Sheriff. Gentlemen. We don't want trouble. Our guests are sleeping."

Sheriff Talmadge stared the manager down. "One of 'em might not be breathing. If he is, we aim to keep him that way."

"Well—"

"What room is Ferwinckle in?"

The manager blinked. "Two-twelve."

"Git." Talmadge motioned with his pistol. "Away. We men have a job to do and you're holding up justice."

The manager scurried behind his desk, and Morgan took the lead. Youth on his side, he was the first to clear the stairs, his boots nearly silent on the thick carpet.

Outside two-twelve, Morgan listened, his ear to the door until Talmadge and Dad arrived. He shook his head—hadn't heard a thing.

He had a *really* bad feeling about this.

The sheriff pressed his ear to the panel, then held up three fingers. Folded one in—two. One.

A well-placed kick—Sheriff Talmadge had done this before—and the door thundered against the inside wall. Light from a single lamp spilled over the scene.

The odor of blood, vomit, sweat, and fear hit Morgan's nostrils.

Two men, one seated and rope wound about his torso and legs made sure he stayed that way. Ferwinckle, but Morgan only knew that because of the suit and once-fastidiously polished shoes he'd been wearing at the jailhouse. His face was swollen, battered and bleeding.

An assailant, a pistol pressed to the tender underside of Ferwinckle's jaw, whipped his head toward the door.

Morgan had the villain in his sights, as did Dad and the sheriff.

"We won't miss," Talmadge informed him, as if saying howdy on the boardwalk at noon to a fellow he liked. "Throw it down, if you want to live."

Ferwinckle moaned.

Faster than a rattler strike, the varmint spun, raised the pistol, and fired.

Morgan ignored the reflex to duck.

More than one target practice prepared two gunsmiths and one lawman to handle the threat.

The collective boom of three firearms

erupting simultaneously nearly deafened.

Whoever he was, the varmint dived for the open window, devoid of a screen, and would have made it, too, had he not gone up against the three best shots in Mountain Home.

Spent powder covered the unpleasant odors, but Morgan's stomach kicked anyway. He'd never intentionally shot a man before. Never had reason to.

"If he ain't dead, I'll eat my hat." Sheriff Talmadge kicked the revolver free of the fallen man. It spun, thumping against the wall.

In the hallway, voices sounded, raised in alarm. Muffled thumps of running feet on carpet.

"He dead?" Morgan had to know. He wouldn't holster his hand-cannon 'til he knew for sure.

Talmadge grunted. "Can't live with one perfect hole in the heart, now can he?"

Had two shots gone wide? One hole?

Ah—three bullets. One hole.

One more look at Wardie's swollen, bruised face and Morgan set aside his doubts. Anybody who'd beat on a man deserved what he got.

Wardie opened his mouth and tried to speak. Two teeth tumbled from his mouth.

"Hard to talk," Talmadge said, "with a broken jaw." The lawman had cut through the ropes binding Wardie Ferwinckle to the chair, "So skip to the important stuff. That yahoo alone? Or are there more we should know about?"

Wardie held up one finger—broken, at an odd angle.

Morgan winced. The boy might not practice dentistry for a good long time.

Dad, always calm in situations like this,

turned to the crowd at the door. "Don't stand there with your mouths open—go get a doctor. Maybe two."

Sixteen

The following afternoon, Zylphia lay in bed, aggravated at Elizabeth Louise's constant badgering.

If Zylphia wanted to come downstairs and socialize with the family, she would have.

If she wanted to be downstairs where temperatures were at least ten degrees cooler, she would have.

If she wanted to come downstairs and allow George to see her—like this...

She choked on emotion too big, too immense.

...she would have.

Didn't Elizabeth Louise comprehend a thing? Zylphia's entire life was stolen from her when that...that *villain* had murdered Elijah and tried to murder Wardie Ferwinckle.

And why? For money.

That hired gun, the one caught in the hotel

and shot to death, accepted money to kill Elijah.

Why? Because Elijah had invested a goodly amount of money with them, anticipating a healthy return. But the investment company had been a fraud—and Elijah had discovered as much.

The hired man had beat sweet Mr. Ferwinckle, forcing him to disclose financial details of the business—and of the Speare family. Turned out the money Ferwinckle had withdrawn and carried all the way to Mountain Home had been planted by the fraudulent investment firm, with the purpose of following Wardie Ferwinckle to Zee and Elizabeth Louise.

Such evil designs. She shivered all over whenever she thought about it.

The sheriff believed the photographs and detailed description of the villain would help other police forces. They'd weigh, measure, describe distinguishing marks, and share all over the country.

All Zee cared about was that the horror behind Elijah's untimely death was somewhat resolved.

"Mother. You cannot remain in bed any longer."

"Elizabeth Louise." Zee fought the tears and attempted—*again*—to dry her eyes. "Please, no more pleading with me to do something I don't want to do. Be a good daughter and sit quietly."

"I'm going downstairs, Mother. You come down when you're ready."

"But—" Stunned, she pushed into a sitting position to better see her daughter's face. Had she misheard? "I can't be alone, Elizabeth. You know that. It's your duty to remain with me. I'm terrorized. I'm grieving."

Elizabeth, beautiful, lovely girl that she was, took both of Zee's hands. Yes, this attention, this closeness was precisely what she needed from her daughter.

"Actually, Mother," Elizabeth said, her tone even, soft, and yet filled with steel. "No."

Zylphia *couldn't* have heard correctly. Elizabeth Louise *never* sassed her mother. "What did you say?"

"I said no. I love you and I've stood by you through everything, but it's time for me to live my own life."

"You—you can't leave me." Panic sliced through Zee's chest. Sobs erupted. She couldn't help it. An attack of hysterics strangled, twisting off her air.

"You're safe now, Mother. That man is dead. He can't hurt you, or anyone you love, ever again."

Fighting to breathe, to shove aside the horrors, the details she couldn't stop thinking of, she had to admit Elizabeth was right.

Wardie Ferwinckle recovered in the nicest room the hotel had to offer, the doctor paying calls three times a day.

Dear, wonderful, patient Geo had seen to it that man, that horrible man, could never hurt her again. He'd risked his safety—his very life—to save Mr. Ferwinckle, and by so doing, had certainly saved her and Elizabeth Louise.

And what did Geo want in return? Only to see her. To hold her hand, to sit at her side, to ensure she was well.

But—

She flung herself back onto the pillows and

covered her tear-stained face with her hands.

If Geo saw her—like this! In her nightgown, eyes red and swollen, hysterical and out of control—he won't show her the love she desperately needed from him. He'd withhold the kindness she needed...

"We have to go." She threw back the sheet, pushed her feet into her house slippers, and dashed to the chest of drawers. "You sneak out the back door. Find a driver to take us—"

"No."

Dumbfounded, she stared at this woman— this woman she didn't know. "What has gotten into you? Why are you so disobedient?"

"Listen to me, Mother. Listen very carefully." Elizabeth put an arm about Zee's shoulders, took her hand in a sweet, tender hold, and walked her to the settee before the window. Together, they sat.

"I know my father would have seen you as you are now and refused to hold you."

A tremendous sob wrenched free from Zee's throat. She slapped a hand tight over her mouth and fought to remain quiet.

"He wouldn't have allowed you to grieve." Elizabeth's gentle touch upon Zee's back gave her a sense of calm—but how could she feel calm? Her daughter, her good girl *refused* help, *refused* the solace she needed...

Just like her father, like Elijah. That man *never* put his arms about her and assured her he loved her, despite her nerves. That man *never* let her talk through her fears. He'd *never* held her hand when she was afraid and assured her he'd take care of things...

...*Not like Geo*. Geo had done all of those

things. And more.

"Everything you want is right here. A man who loves you. A daughter who loves you."

Zee surged to her feet. "I have to go."

"Do you?"

"Yes, I do." She made it to the chest of drawers before Elizabeth was there, naughty girl, holding her hands and preventing her from finding something to wear.

"You know how badly it hurt when Father died and left you, though he didn't mean to. Mr. Hudson *still* feels that pain. Do you want to do that to him, again?"

Zee's tears erupted, again.

"He loves you." Elizabeth put her arms around Zee and held on. "Why are you scared to stay, accept that he loves you, and be happy?"

"I've—" She fought for air. "Ruined everything. I-I already told him I'm...I'm leaving."

"So change your mind. March over to the first house, hug him, and beg his forgiveness."

"I don't know how! I don't know how to ask anyone to love me—I've tried, my whole life, I've tried. And I've always done it badly because no one ever loved me."

"Mother—stop. Listen to yourself. You know that's not true. You don't need to ask for love. People love you back, simply because of who you are and because you loved them first."

"No."

"Father loved you, but he couldn't express love the way you needed."

Angry, Zee dashed away the tears clinging to her eyelashes.

"Your sons love you. You loved Junior,

Sidney, and me—you loved us first. And we love you."

Zee shrugged. But at least the tears had slowed.

"My brothers love you—and they grew into men. It's only natural for men to leave their mothers and make their own way in the world. They were simply ready to live lives of their own. At their ages, they well should. And me too. I'm age 26. It's time for me to live my own life."

Truth *hurt*.

Like the dickens.

She'd held this daughter back, prevented her from finding love and companionship and a family of her own—all because she'd been too scared to let go of the family she'd so desperately wanted.

"If you want to leave, I won't stop you." Elizabeth stood and walked to the door. Grace and dignity. Confidence and strength. "You're wrong to go, but I won't stop you. You're allowed to make your own decisions."

At the door, Elizabeth waited, but Zee couldn't find the words. How could she admit she'd been wrong? How could she beg Elizabeth Louise's forgiveness?

"I'm staying here, with Morgan." Elizabeth opened the door. "If you were brave, you'd stay too."

With that, she shut the door, softly.

Zee gasped in outrage.

But she hadn't any right to that emotion. Nor did she have a right to the disappointment she'd clung to. She'd done a very bad thing.

Zee rushed to the door, wrenched it open. The hallway was empty—had her baby girl gone so quickly? Rushed outside, to the first house, and into the arms of the man she loved? "I'm sorry, Elizabeth!"

She rushed down the hallway, toward the staircase. "I hurt you. I loved you more than you can possibly imagine, and I hurt you." She picked up the hem of her robe, and hurried down the stairs. "Most of those beaus weren't good enough for you! Some were terrible, like that Raymond Cresswell."

Breathing heavily, she burst into the entry hall, and found her daughter leaning against the front door, tears streaming silently down her cheeks.

"Oh, Elizabeth." She took one halting step toward her daughter, then two. "And some of them *were*. Good enough for you." Pain. So much pain—in her heart, in her head, in her very soul.

Had she ever been in such a state?

With great care, she took Elizabeth Louise's beautiful face between her hands and searched her daughter's blue eyes. "Will you forgive me?"

She nodded. "Yes."

"So easily?"

"You're my mother, and I love you." Elizabeth's hug was certain and powerful and full of healing.

Would Geo forgive her so easily? Only one way to find out.

"Wash your face, Mother. Bathe. Dress your hair, and put on that lovely pale green dress. You will go with me and visit Mr. Hudson. You will let him see for himself that you're well. He'll be over the moon when he realizes you've changed your mind and the wedding is on."

"I have? Changed my mind?"

"Absolutely."

Seventeen

With her mother at her side, Elizabeth raised her hand to knock. Before she'd rapped even once, the door of the first house opened and they were nearly run over by two Hudson men in a hurry.

Elizabeth searched Morgan's features, soaked up every line and curve and hollow of his dear face. Long shadows cast by the setting sun sent golden sheets of sunlight through Morgan's hair, putting her in mind of an archangel.

Last night had been all about business, with the shooting and all that came after it. Photographing the dead man and seeing the corpse under lock and key at the undertaker. The sheriff had a feeling the varmint was on more than one wanted poster.

Tonight was about family. And love. And salvaging anything that remained from the ashes.

"Ladies?" Mr. Hudson said, bowing slightly to

each of them in turn. "We see you have something on your mind. Would you care to come in?"

Mother nodded, then immediately shook her head no.

"Do you mind if we come out?" Mr. Hudson truly was a remarkable man—just what Mother needed.

If she could change...

Elizabeth stepped back, giving them egress.

Last night, about this time, Morgan had vehemently refused to marry her. Despite that, the time had come to lay herself bare, and take the risk of a lifetime.

Morgan would never laugh at her expense, but he'd also never do what he didn't want to do. She couldn't find the words to so much as begin.

Speaking with him, telling him everything that was in her heart, had seemed like a good idea, until now...

She glanced at Mother, who took baby-steps toward Mr. Hudson. "Geo?"

Mr. Hudson opened his arms and Mother threw herself into his embrace. Mother sobbed, Mr. Hudson squeezed her tight and kissed her brow. "Don't go, Zee. I love you. Don't you see that?"

Mother laughed through her tears. "I love you, Geo. Can you forgive me?"

"Darling Zee, all is forgiven. Say you'll stay and marry me."

Elizabeth clamped a hand over her mouth. Just like that—in the exchange of thirty seconds, Mother and soon-to-be stepdad had said exactly what she couldn't find words to say.

Bless Morgan's generous heart. She saw the

moment he decided to make this as easy on her as possible. How she *loved* him.

He drew near, touched her waist and her jaw, tipping her face up to his. "Let's leave the sweethearts alone, shall we?" He spoke near her temple, his breath a caress.

Surely he wouldn't touch her like this...as if they were more than friends, more than soon-to-be siblings, if he didn't want another chance. Would he?

Her heart pounded and her tongue stuck to the roof of her mouth. He'd barely escorted her around the corner of the first house when he caught her up in his arms and kissed her.

With *more* desperation, *more* intensity than the first time—if that were possible.

"We have something special, you and I." He stole another kiss. This one brief and emphatic. Like an exclamation point. "You can't deny it."

"You did."

Confusion interrupted his train of thought. "I what?"

"You denied it. You kissed me, like that, the sheriff saw us, and you adamantly refused to marry me."

"A mistake. And I regret it. I'm a man, Lizzy. That means I'm going to say and do stupid things now and again. But one thing's for certain—I'd wed you right now. This instant."

Wed? Shouldn't they finish making up first?

Her stomach lifted and seemed to tangle up with her heart. She couldn't find a single word to respond to that ridiculous non-proposal.

She'd never actually heard a proposal of marriage in her rather poor experience, but that didn't seem to be a very good one.

"But you deserve a courtship, attention, a wedding of your own. Last thing I'm fool enough to do is expect you to share your wedding with your mother. And my Dad."

She opened her mouth, entirely unsure what to say. Nothing came out.

"I know that's foolish. Arrah, selfish creature that she's always been, would've insisted on her *own* everything, her *due*." He shook his head as if trying to clear the mental image of that spoiled woman—what *had* he ever seen in her?

"But... I..." She shrugged, utterly lost. "I don't know much about proposals of marriage, mind you, but I don't think a man is supposed to compare me to the woman he'd almost married."

"I'm doing this badly, aren't I?"

"What are you trying to do? I don't know if you *are* proposing."

"I'm trying to explain." He shook off what had to be aggravation.

So, this wasn't a proposal?

She tried to slip free, but Morgan held on tighter. "Don't go, Lizzy. Stay here in Mountain Home with me. Be my wife. I don't think I could stand it if I had to live with you as a sister."

She giggled. Had to be the relief, the utter rightness of hearing him actually say marriage— well, he hadn't actually said marriage, but that's what he'd meant.

"I mean it." His brows drew together.

"I know."

"Marry me, Lizzy."

"Was that a question?"

He rested his forehead against hers. "Just like

I can't stand other people telling me what to do, I'm not real fond of teasing. Now would be a good time to say yes."

"Yes."

She sealed that promise with a kiss. A sweet, tender, genuine kiss. One she hoped conveyed just how much she'd come to love him.

She slipped her fingers into his hair, warm and soft, where it lay over his collar. He smelled of sunshine-dried cotton, bay rum, minty tooth powder, gun oil, and man.

Morgan Hudson smelled like happily forever after.

"Your mother lost her marbles over the guns inherent in gunsmithing. You lost your father to gunfire. Tell me right now if you won't be a gunsmith's bride."

"And if I object to your trade? What would you do?"

"I'd—" He blinked. He swallowed, hard. The man loved his work. He was born for it—a natural, like his father and his father before him.

She stroked a thumb over his beard stubble, loving the texture. He obviously didn't know how smitten she was with him. He had as many insecurities as she—and that must cease. If they were to be stronger, together, happier because of their bond, she must help him shed his doubts and build his confidence. "I love *you*, Morgan Hudson. I'd love you if you were a gunslinger, a lawman, an executioner, or an undertaker."

Light radiated from his smile. Boy howdy, the man was more than gorgeous when he smiled. "Morbid thoughts."

She chuckled. "You started it, referencing

Mother's hysterics over guns and Father's death to violence."

"So...you do have a problem with a gunsmith?" That amazing smile began to creep back onto his features. "I could learn to sling iron. Might have to move to Cañon City, but I might find work executing at the State Penitentiary."

How could the man keep a straight face? "You'd better be teasing."

He lost that smile then, somberness chasing away all frivolity. "I killed that man. The one who nearly killed Ferwinckle."

"In self-defense. The sheriff and your father shot too. Talmadge said he shot at you first."

"True."

Gratitude filled her, overflowing even as tears blurred her vision. "Mr. Ferwinckle and Sheriff Talmadge believe the hired gun was the one who shot and killed my father in St. Louis."

"I know."

"Thank you. Mother and I were in danger, could have lost our lives without warning, and we didn't suspect it. You might have acted in self-defense, but you saved our lives."

Moments slipped past while she fought to control her emotion. "I'll always be grateful. If you couldn't handle a gun, I'd have lost you." Her throat closed and she fought to regain her ability to speak. "He would have come after Mother and me next."

He pressed a lingering kiss to her forehead. The kind of kiss that made her feel cherished, valued, and *needed*.

"I love you." His whispered declaration evoked tingles along every nerve.

"I love you, Morgan Hudson."

"That means we are out of options." His beautifully expressive face disclosed joy, happiness, determination, confidence, and limitless love.

How had their parents' romance brought them together? She never would have believed it possible. "What do we do now?"

"Only one thing we can do."

Her belly tingled. She wanted romantic words. A marriage offer worthy of telling and retelling to children and grandchildren.

"I never thought I'd see a blessing the size of the great state of Colorado come from the loss of my mother, but it happened. Her life ended too early, but started a course of events that ultimately brought you to me. Now that I've found you, I'm not willing to let you go." He loosened his hold, eased back a step, as if he'd drop to one knee. So very story-book romance.

But instead, he tightened his embrace.

Disappointed? How could she be? This man wanted her, in his arms.

One more lingering kiss, then Morgan swept a thumb over her lower lip. "Will you be my wife, Lizzy Lou Speare? Take my name and become Elizabeth Louise Hudson?"

"I'd be honored."

He whooped with joy.

"Morgan?"

"Hmm?"

"I prefer Lizzy."

Eighteen

Morgan claimed one more heady kiss as Mrs. Speare appeared around the side of the house, her hand clutched in Dad's. The pair of lovers had obviously made up well and good, if the smiles on their faces were a trusted indication.

After all, those smiles did not fade, despite catching Morgan kissing Lizzy with enthusiasm.

"Oh, just what I wanted!" Mrs. Speare practically pulled her daughter out of Morgan's embrace.

This stepmother/mother-in-law combination would be a challenge.

For Lizzy, he'd manage.

Not that he'd admit it easily, but Zylphia Speare, soon to be Zylphia Hudson, despite her quirks, was a woman far too much like himself. Not a comfortable realization, but Lizzy had been right.

Understanding Zee had made all the difference.

"Mother?" Lizzy hugged Zee in return, then pulled back to discreetly tuck a lock of her mother's hair back into a pin. Dad, apparently, had made up for lost time.

"I'm thrilled to see you two kissing and making up." Zee sounded delighted. "I'd love nothing more than to see you two wedded to one another in the same ceremony uniting Geo and me."

Morgan's attention hadn't left his bride's face—so he noticed her hesitancy. She'd been placating her mother for twenty years. It'd take time, but eventually, he'd help her ease back into a healthy amount of following her mother's edicts.

"No time to waste," Zee continued. "I want grandchildren."

"Mother!" Lizzy's face flushed. *Adorable*.

Morgan fought the urge to laugh. He'd warned his bride he'd make mistakes, but hoped to avoid one that serious until he'd placed his ring on her finger and she was his, forever.

Some mistakes wouldn't be laughing matters at all. He'd try to avoid disappointing her altogether. Every day. For the rest of their lives. She deserved that, and more.

Dad clapped Morgan on the back. "Stand up for me, Son?"

"And I'll stand up for you, Lizzy." Zee talked over Dad—something she came by naturally. Why stop now?

Dad didn't seem the slightest bit troubled. He'd never looked happier. Not even...*before*. The realization impinged on the buoyant joy salvaged from the ashes. Having seen both, up close and personal, he had no interest in returning there.

From now on, he chose happiness. Optimism, living, and loving—and always with Lizzy Lou in the middle of that picture.

Deep in his heart, he had no doubt his mother would be pleased Dad had found love again. She'd loved Dad 'til her dying breath. She'd not have wanted his life to end, just because hers had.

Silently, he promised his angel mother he'd be happy for Dad too.

His mother would be overjoyed he'd finally found the love of his life. She'd have loved Lizzy.

"I want to share my special—*our* special day." Zee took both of Lizzy's hands, squeezed tight. Happy tears ran down her cheeks and dripped from her chin. "What do you say?"

Lizzy glanced at Morgan, a question in her eyes. As if she'd do whatever he wanted.

Everybody knew weddings were entirely a woman's affair. "Whatever you want, Lizzy. I'd marry you anytime, anywhere, with or without a joint ceremony. I just want to marry you. Officially, legally, forever."

That won him one of her quick, genuine smiles. Like the day they'd met, on the train platform, and he'd thought her widowed and the mother of two monster children.

"Oh!" Zee caught a tremulous breath. "I told you, Geo. Didn't I? I *knew* our children were right for each other. We're going to be one big, gloriously happy family."

"Are you sure?" Lizzy asked, searching Morgan's eyes, uncertainty showing in her posture and her voice. He'd enjoy helping the strong, confident Lizzy emerge. That Lizzy was in there, somewhere.

"I'm sure, darling. Entirely up to you."

That won him another quick smile. Rich and sincere, a quick one-two punch to the gut. He *loved* making her smile.

"Then yes, Mother. A double wedding it will be."

"Wonderful!" Zee squeezed Lizzy tight, then opened her arms to Morgan.

He'd fought off every hug Zylphia Speare had attempted to inflict upon him from the day she'd arrived.

Lizzy's smile morphed to a pucker, making her feelings on the matter clear. Rejecting this hug would not win him any favors from his bride-to-be. He grinned at Lizzy and put his arms about her mother. He squeezed her tight and allowed her time to hug him back.

Mother-in-law seemed a much more tolerable relationship to Zylphia Speare Hudson than that of stepmother. Mother-in-law, he could live with. "Congratulations, Mother."

Zee caught her breath. "Did you hear that, Elizabeth Louise?"

Lizzy nodded, love shining in her magnificent blue eyes. "Yes, Mother. I heard him use the magic word."

"He called me Mother!"

"Indeed he did." Dad sounded like a proud papa.

This was a good day. Both Hudson men ready to move forward to the next chapter of their lives. They wouldn't have to forget Tildie—no need at all. Two secure, well-loved, and confident women loved those Hudson men, memories and all.

Surprising though it was, it seemed Morgan's heart had enough room to wholly love the right woman...*and* her peculiar mother.

Zee sniffed, blew her nose into her hankie, and smiled. "Run along you two. Brush your hair, Elizabeth Louise, and pin it up. We're leaving in ten minutes to apply for marriage licenses, then calling upon Pastor Gilbert immediately thereafter."

Now?

He wanted to marry Lizzy—but *now?*

Women were in charge of these things...because these things took time. Dresses needed sewing. Invitations in fancy handwriting on thick cream-colored paper shipped all the way from New York City. Somebody had to cook an elaborate meal for guests.

He'd heard all about it as Arrah had planned the most absurdly ornate wedding. Mountain Home residents wouldn't have known what to do with all that fluff and nonsense.

That necessary time for preparations had saved him. Without it, he might have actually married Arrah. He shivered, realizing how close he'd come to a tragedy.

He'd dodged a bullet when she'd called off that wedding and left his engagement ring behind.

Ring.

He couldn't wed Lizzy without a ring.

He opened the kitchen door for the ladies who swept inside, tittering with excitement.

Everybody knew the ring was part of the ceremony—and an important part at that. He had *ten* minutes.

No cigar band for Lizzy Lou. And no bent nail,

either.

He caught Dad's sleeve, then waited for the women to move beyond hearing. "I want to give Lizzy Mother's wedding ring."

"She would have wanted that too."

Dad braced a hand on Morgan's shoulder and squeezed. One of those precious father-son moments that had become so rare. Perhaps all the more valued because of the infrequency.

"Let's get you that ring."

Morgan shouldn't have been surprised Dad led the way to the first house, rather than the new.

Nineteen

Epilogue

March 13, 1888
Almost three years later...

Morgan Hudson had never seen March weather so severe, so extreme, or so debilitating.

Because of the blizzard, he'd moved his wife into the big house with their parents, to conserve firewood. No sense heating two stoves and two kitchens.

Morgan had been out on snowshoes, during breaks in the storm, along with other men, ensuring individuals and families in Mountain Home were safe—and taking care of those in need.

He'd paid a visit to Miss Ina Dimond—whoops. Make that Miss Ina and her new husband of all of two weeks. They'd not had time to get settled, chop adequate firewood...and living with Cousin Ray Cresswell and his bride had put a strain on the resources.

The day had been rewarding, fulfilling, and downright bone-chilling. He'd never been so glad to be home, huddled close to the stove with his three favorite people. He held a cup of coffee between two chapped hands and soaked up the warmth.

"Since when," Mother asked, "have Colorado winters been this severe?"

Yes, Mother was anxious about the blizzard, but then, so was everybody else in the valley. She'd tempered over the three years—almost—since she'd come to Colorado. Morgan figured Dad had worked that significant change.

They'd been so good for each other—Dad and Mother.

And Morgan could say, without hesitation, that he and Lizzy had been good for each other too.

"Come sit down to supper." Mother set a heavy Dutch oven in the middle of the kitchen table. They'd shut off the rooms they weren't immediately using, heating only those needed. At bedtime, they'd move their mattresses close to the kitchen range and camp on the floor.

Not his idea of a good time, but doing so served the purpose of keeping an eye on their aging parents *and* staying warm. The storm would pass, and things—well, most things—would go back to the way they'd been.

"Morgan? Will you say grace?"

With his wife's hand in his right, and Mother's in his left, Morgan offered a prayer of gratitude for shelter, comfort, and plenty to eat. His mother's ring, upon Lizzy's finger, reminded him of the gifts in his life.

Life was good.

"Amen."

Amens all around, and the conversation returned to the snow. The parents had never stopped urging Morgan and Lizzy to move into the big house, but they'd loved their solitude, their privacy. But this winter, they'd weather the late spring serious storms, together.

And as summer came around—if it did—the young Mr. and Mrs. Hudson just might remain in the big house.

"You know we can't manage the stairs any longer." Mother dished up steaming baked beans and ham, rich, fragrant, and hot. "You know how Dad's arthritic back is when the weather is disagreeable."

Morgan shared a secret smile with Lizzy.

"If you move in," Mother continued, "you young people could have the entire upstairs to yourselves. Dad and I will move our bedroom down, and use that little room behind the kitchen for our own. It will suit our needs more than adequately."

Morgan held his wife's eye and smiled. He gave her a nod. The timing was perfect.

"That's a fine idea, Mother."

"It is?" Zee dropped her fork. "Why is it a fine idea?"

She didn't dare hope—he saw that much clearly on her face.

"It's a grand idea." Morgan couldn't help but grinning, wide as could be. He squeezed his wife's hand. "It'll be better for the baby to be near his grandparents."

Who knew four people could make so much joyful noise?

Outside, the storm raged, the wind howled, and if they were looking through the windows into the gloom, they'd have wondered what they could be happy about.

But within that warm kitchen, during the worst storm of the century, Morgan Hudson's heart overflowed with contentment.

"When?" Mother demanded. "When will the little one arrive?"

"By Thanksgiving."

Blessed, perfect timing.

Morgan lifted Lizzy's fingers to his lips, kissed her knuckles and lingered. He smiled into her eyes. "By Thanksgiving," he repeated.

More accurately, late October or early November, but it seemed wise to add a few weeks, just in case Mother lost her patience.

"Most wonderful gift you could give us," Mother insisted, as she hugged her daughter. "Me! A grandmother!" Her eyes rounded as tears welled and spilled. "Our grandchild, Geo. *Our* grandchild."

Zee's happiness, in our own odd ways, became Morgan's happiness, and the greater he understood his mother-in-law, the more he sought to make her happy.

"You'll teach him everything you know about gunsmithing, won't you?" Mother's attention bounced from Dad to Morgan to Dad again.

"When it's time." Morgan couldn't help but smile.

"You *must*! The Hudsons *need* a fifth generation of gunsmiths."

The conversation swept off onto the path of Mother's choosing, and Morgan finished his meal, filling his belly with the hot, hardy food. His heart, full to the brim, basked in the warmth of his parents' home, sublimely unconcerned with the raging storm outside.

Please *share* this book with a friend.
Paperbacks are easy to lend.

Please *recommend* this book.
*Please share your thoughts on this book
with friends.*

Please post a *review.*
*Reviews from readers make all the difference to
those browsing and buying, as well as to writers.
Please take a moment and leave an honest review.
One short sentence will do.*

To Review *The Gunsmith's Bride* Online:

One Quick Click =
one page links you to all review sites
(stores where you might have purchased this title,
and exclusive review sites like Goodreads and
BookBub).

Simply type in:

www.kristinholt.com/14058-2

(not case-sensitive, but
dashes/hyphens are required)

Or scan the QR code.

Note: all bold-face words or phrases are links in the kindle edition—and connect to a wealth of background and historical information. If you're interested, please visit

www.kristinholt.com/history-the-gunsmiths-bride *(or scan the QR code)*

to view this same content <u>with clickable links</u>.

Thank you for reading The Gunsmith's Bride. I'm delighted to have had the chance to share this story with you. Now, I want to give you a peek "behind the scenes", at the accurate history that supported Morgan and Elizabeth's romance in Mountain Home.

You'll find articles I've written about the related history (with more to come!) on my website (and a few blog articles I've published on other sites), with easy-to-follow, clickable links here: **www.KristinHolt.com/book-description-the-gunsmiths-bride**. Capital letters don't matter, but dashes *do*, and Kristin must be spelled *e-free*.

When I wrote this novella, I'd committed to include it in the five-novella bundle titled GUNSMOKE & GINGHAM. I wanted to ensure both "gunsmoke" and "gingham" had a role in my tale. The **"gingham"** part was easier for me, as I've been sewing since I was about age 11. My mother sews beautifully, and taught me, a little at a time, until I was quite able to sew my entire wardrobe by junior high. Thus I certainly know what gingham is...but **historically, I discovered, gingham was so much more than the checked pattern we recognize** in red-and-white tablecloths. It seemed fitting, given Elizabeth's comfort at the outset of the story, that a gingham dress would be her "best dress", and she'd wear hers at **the celebration of Independence Day**.

The "gunsmoke" part of the equation required much more research for me. I love the research component of writing fiction, so studying **the work of a gunsmith in the mid- to late-nineteenth century** was far from grueling. But I wanted more than a gunsmith. I enjoyed planning ways that literal gunsmoke—from the firing of an era-specific pistol or rifle—would add to the story. Not only were **shooting contests** a standard event at seasonal events in the American West, but adding this contest is a nod at the *gunsmoke*. Please see my blog articles (easy links to click through) on **my website's page for *The Gunsmith's Bride***, as provided in my second paragraph, above.

Names like George, Elizabeth, and Morgan are well known, and very appropriate for the birthdates of my characters. I use information such as census reports and websites compiling common names of babies born in the United States within certain Victorian five- or ten-year spans. But the name Zylphia? Made up, right? Nope. Quite common for a woman of her age, as is her intimate nickname, Zee. **The practice of giving Morgan his mother's maiden name** for his "Christian name" (first name) was another Victorian common practice. Later on, giving sons the mother's maiden name as a middle name became more common, presently reverting back to the practice of mother's-maiden-name-for-first-name option.

When it comes to creating a fictitious town, but ensuring stories are still set in a very real place, writers do well to pay attention to little things like types of trees, weather, temperatures, and more. While researching details such as these, for my fictitious town of Mountain Home (set in the Rocky Mountains west of Denver, Colorado), I came across the **horrific weather of the 1880s**. Not just the "Schoolhouse Blizzard" and **Great NYC Blizzard(s) of 1888**, nor "The Snow Winter"/Long Winter of 1880-81 when the term "blizzard" was actually first used in reference to snow and weather (because those who lived then had never seen nor heard of such horrific snowfall, weather, and natural consequences. The entire decade of the 1880s will be remembered in history as one continual devastating storm after devastating storm. Please **see that article** and enjoy!

I intentionally set this story in the summer, to ensure the Speare women could get through to Colorado, from Missouri (the pictures you'll see in **my "Blizzards of 1880s" article** show the snow plowed from the tracks, heaped as high as the engine and cars on either side), as well as the frontier traditions of contests (including shooting), picnics, social gatherings, fireworks (oh, yes!), and more.

One element of nineteenth century life, true-to-history, that I couldn't resist writing into the conflict of this book, was the **sad reality of depression**. I'm alarmed at what really happened to individuals who suffered from mental illness, even through the mid-twentieth century. Lobotomies. **Confinement in asylums.**

Severely abusive "treatments". And *so* much worse.

Several reviewers of this title, within the anthology where it first appeared, mentioned how the reader really didn't like Zylphia early on, but understood her far better as the story progressed. Yes! Exactly what I'd hoped would happen. Zee was a difficult woman to like. Self-centered. Manipulative. Demanding. And yes, suffering from depression. In today's world, individuals can and do receive help from trained professionals, including medicinal help, and can live quite normal lives. Poor Zee... And poor Elizabeth, who bore the brunt of her mother's manipulation.

Also true to Victorian-American societal expectation were silly (as far as twenty-first century people see things) laws such as **"No Kissing!"**. Such laws really were on the books of townships, towns, communities, etc. Victorians were rather proper, buttoned-up folk, and they tended to enforce such rules in "polite society". I really enjoyed writing the article called **"Law Forbidding Kissing on the streets of Mountain Home?"**—as I shared numerous vintage newspaper articles from the era, illustrating how some truly saw kissing in public as abhorrent (but not all did), the beliefs of some who thought unmarried women should remain chased and never-kissed until *at* the altar, and more! I hope you'll stop by and read it.

My warmest thanks for reading *The Gunsmith's Bride*. I hope you found both the story and a peek at the historical setting of this novella to be enjoyable. You're invited to visit **my website page for the *Holidays in Mountain Home* series [http://www.kristinholt.com/holidays-in-mountain-home-series]** to explore other titles in this loosely related series (where each title stands alone). As this instance shows, not all "holiday" books are about Christmas.

With warmest appreciation,

Kristin

HOLIDAYS IN MOUNTAIN HOME
Series

In Chronological Order:

Courting Miss Cartwright (Rocky & Felicity), **1879**
Book 5, Founder's Day NOVELLA

This Noelle (Phil & Caroline), **1881**
Prequel: Book 0.5, Christmas NOVELLA

The Gunsmith's Bride (Morgan & Elizabeth), **1885**
Book 6, Independence Day NOVELLA

Unmistakably Yours (Hank & Jane, Oscar & Ina),
1887
Book 8, Thanksgiving NOVEL

Home for Christmas (Hunter & Miranda), **1898**
Book 1, Christmas NOVELLA

Maybe This Christmas (Luke & Effie), **1899**
Book 2, Christmas NOVELLA

The Witching Eve (Gus & Noelle), **1900**
Title 7, Halloween SHORT STORY

The Marshal's Surrender (Gus & Noelle), **1900**
Book 3, Christmas NOVEL

The Drifter's Proposal (Malloy & Adaline), **1900**
Book 4, Christmas NOVELLA

http://www.kristinholt.com/holidays-in-mountain-home-series

P.S. to find my page:

www.kristinholt.com/holidays-in-mountain-home-series

more quickly, see:

http://bit.ly/2A754ZY
(case sensitive)

or scan this code:

Books by Kristin Holt

www.KristinHolt.com/books

And while you're there, please sign up for her newsletter. *Be the first to hear about new releases, sales, and subscriber-only extras.*

Learn more about Kristin Holt's Series:

THE HUSBAND-MAKER TRILOGY

PROSPERITY'S MAIL-ORDER BRIDES

SIX BRIDES FOR SIX GIDEONS

HOLIDAYS IN MOUNTAIN HOME

And **collaborative works** ~

USA TODAY Bestselling Author

KRISTIN HOLT

Hi! I'm Kristin Holt, *USA Today* bestselling author of Sweet Romances (G- and PG-rated) set in the Victorian American West.

While secular in nature, my titles are "Appropriate for All Audiences" and appeal to selective readers and fans of Christian historical romance.

I write frequent articles (or *view recent posts easily* on my Home Page, www.KristinHolt.com, *scroll down*) about the **nineteenth century American west—every subject of possible interest to readers**, amateur historians, authors...as all of these tidbits surfaced while researching for my books. I also blog monthly at *Sweet Americana Sweethearts* and *Sweet Romance Reads.* You'll find links to my blog posts and a wealth of information on my website:

www.KristinHolt.com

I love to hear from readers! Please drop me a note:

www.KristinHolt.com/contact-kristin

(Kristin is e-free.)

Or find me on Facebook:

www.facebook.com/KristinHoltSweetVicto rianWesternRomance/ *(Kristin is e-free)*

You're invited to join a fantastic Facebook group for authors and readers of Western Historical Romances (of all heat levels), Pioneer Hearts.

www.Facebook.com/groups/pioneerhearts

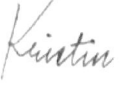